D1560274

FAIRY TALE VILLAINS REIMAGINED

Susan Bianculli   Jeanne Kramer-Smyth
Ameria Lewis   Pamela McNamee   Laura Ring
Judy Rubin   Hope Erica Schultz
Madeline Smoot   C.H. Spalding

CBaY Books
Dallas, Texas

Stepmothers & the Big Bad Wolf:
Fairy Tale Villains Reimagined
Edited by Madeline Smoot

Text Copyright © 2014
Forest Image Copyright © shutterstock.com/Baksiabat
Queen Image Copyright © shutterstock.com/SusIO
Wolf Image Copyright © shutterstock.com/Ksanawo

For more information, write:
CBAY Books
PO Box 670296
Dallas, TX 75367

Children's Brains are Yummy Books
Austin, Texas
www.cbaybooks.com

For CPSIA compliance, see our website
at www.cbaybooks.com.

Printed in the United States of America.

ISBN: 978-1-933767-40-6
ISBN: 978-1-933767-41-3 (ebook)

Table of Contents

Soteli Ma
Laura Ring

The court astrologers said a great cataclysm was coming—an alignment of stars and planets not seen since the demon Ravana stole Sita from the hand of Lord Rama. We didn't pay much attention. My father's advisors were always warning of something: Famine. Plague. Invaders from beyond the Black Waters.

But in the months that followed, strange rumors began to spread—sightings of monsters, shapeshifters, a giant carp that sprouted human lips, warning of "nets that will block out the sun;" a fig tree with human arms that seized peasant children, fresh from their bath in the Yamuna. The people talked of *rakshasas*, *deos*—demonic spirits long consigned to the pages of books, to the tapestries hanging on the palace walls. My father dismissed the talk as fancy or fear-mongering.

Then one day, we noticed that the palace djinns were gone. They no longer hovered on the terrace at dusk to say their prayers or raced on the rooftops, knocking over tiles and upsetting planters. No one

1

could remember the djinns leaving before.

We should have paid attention. But we did not. Summer passed. Farmers brought in the monsoon harvest. Revenue collectors collected. Court life continued as always, with feasts and games, weddings, and the royal hunt.

On the 10th day of Rajab, my good father the king rode out with a hunting party on the trail of a white tiger. When his arrow struck the beast, it transformed into a demoness—a *rakshasi* as tall as the surrounding banyan trees. She struck down my father with one swipe of her taloned hand, and by week's end, I found myself in a wood-and-thatch hut, at the edge of the kingdom, with Soteli Ma.

When my lady mother died five years ago, my father did not lack for comfort. All the courtesans in the palace waited to take my mother's place, just as they waited fruitlessly while she lived, to join her as co-wife in the royal quarters. I do not know why he married a nameless girl from the eastern hills, who spoke not a single word during her seven-day wedding and then left the palace never to return. Even a child could see that she was beautiful, in the way that wild things sometimes can be. But she lacked the graces of a noblewoman of the court. She was gifted neither in dancing, nor singing, nor, as I was to discover, conversation.

When my father's steward deposited me without explanation or ceremony at my stepmother's door, Soteli Ma stood stone-faced and silent until the carriage and riders were out of sight.

"So your father is dead," she said.

Without another word, she stripped the ornaments from my limbs—the gold bracelets, the strings of lapis lazuli.

"You are no longer a princess."

I reach up my hand to touch the jagged frill of hair floating around my suddenly weightless head. My long black braid—my future husband's bounty—is gone, along with my silk sari and slippers. She leaves me my dagger though, tied to my left calf with strips of brown leather. It is a sign of my status: decorative, useless really. Soteli Ma smirks when she sees it, when the last of the unwrapped sari falls to the ground.

"What's your name?" she asks. As if she doesn't know.

"Rania Shah Sultan Begum," I answer.

Soteli Ma tosses my braid on the cooking fire and

gathers the silk in her arms.

"That's a name for a princess," she says. "Your name is Chakoo." Little blade.

It is hard to picture my father in this rude wooden hovel, the skirt of his silk *kurta* spread across the coarse jute bed. He left nothing of himself here—no Tabrizi carpet, no silver *paan-daan*. No child. I am glad. My loathing can be absolute.

Soteli Ma locks me in the cellar again. I no longer cringe from the damp, earthen roots stretching like fingers from the ceiling, the skittering of stick legs fleeing my bare feet. The first time she shut me in, I pounded on the wooden door and cried for light—a candle, an oil lamp. Soteli Ma stuffed rags under the door, denying me even a sliver of sun.

"Get used to the dark," she said.

There is nothing to sit on but maggoty soil. I stand. I can stand for hours now, without moving, without making a sound. In my mind, I catalog the crimes of Soteli Ma and devise punishment.

I look foul. I smell foul. If the nobles of the court

could see me now, they would not recognize me. My corner of the hut is bare, bereft of decoration or soft surfaces. Straw mat. Homespun *kurta*. And a mirror—for no matter how tightly I hold to my former life, Soteli Ma finds countless ways to remind me that it is gone.

Soteli Ma has a larder full of food—root vegetables, herbs, grains, dried beans—but I am not allowed to eat it. Soteli Ma points me to the woods and tells me I can eat what I can forage. I vomit for days after eating berries from a flowering bush and suffer two nights of visions after a meal of spotted toadstools. I am careful now. I know what to gather and what to avoid.

In the early days, I would dream of Eid-day feasts: lamb with almonds, pheasant on the bone, honeyed milk with pistachios. In my hunger, I would chew tree bark until my lips were black. I cried the first time I killed a rabbit—as much for myself as for the poor creature that touched its nose to my hand as if I really were a princess: someone who stands apart from the business of survival.

Now I trap and kill game without thought or ceremony. I'm sure this pleases Soteli Ma, for she welcomes my degradation.

I am running beside a stream at the tree line. My bare feet step lightly on the moss-covered path, untroubled by the press of thorns or pebbles. I am fast. I am lighter than the leaf of a neem tree. It is the only time, since coming to Soteli Ma's, that I am happy.

Of course we played games in the palace gardens. We battled with kites, danced with our cousins, and spied on our elders.

But I had never run like this before.

The first time was less than a fortnight after my arrival. Though I harbored no illusions that Soteli Ma looked on me as a daughter, I never believed she wished me dead—until the day I sneaked a vial of lavender oil from the larder and washed two weeks of dirt, stench and pitch from my aching body in the nearby stream. When I returned to the hut, Soteli Ma stared at me, her eyes dark.

"You stupid girl," she said, between clenched teeth. I backed out of the hut, confused and afraid. When she followed, instinct took over, and I ran. Soteli Ma chased after me.

"You're right to run, Chakoo," she shouted. "You better hope that I don't catch you."

I ran until my feet bled—until my legs gave way and I collapsed in the billowing dirt. Soteli Ma looked down at me with grim satisfaction, and from then on, such has been my punishment for any infraction: I run, and Soteli Ma gives chase.

I take a secret pleasure in my growing speed and stamina, the feeling that I can run forever, that I can leave everything behind. I keep this secret to myself, lest Soteli Ma discover it and contrive to take it away from me.

In the early days, I expected my late father's retinue to return and bring me back to the palace. I listened for horses and riders, certain that I didn't belong in this place, that I hadn't been abandoned by the ones I loved. I was entirely cut off from external events. Soteli Ma went to market every week without me, and any news she received of the court or the wider world, she refused to share.

I knew nothing of the state of the kingdom—who lived, who died, who held the throne. I longed for news of the growing threat that the court sages had prophesied. *Rakshasa*s, *deo*s—whatever their name, they were evil, with evil purpose. There would be no placating them, no reasoning with them. War was coming. My father had not believed it. And now he was dead.

"How do you stop a *rakshasa*?" I ask.

We gather sticks in the forest, and I voice my thoughts aloud.

Soteli Ma rarely speaks, so it is always a surprise when she does. She drops her bundle on the ground, retrieving one stick in her hand. She points at a neem tree on the far side of a clearing.

"Do you see that knot on the trunk?"

I squint and nod. Soteli Ma draws back her arm and hurls the stick at the tree; it bounces off the knot with a clack.

"Now you," she says.

We throw sticks at the neem tree for hours. By nightfall, I am hitting the knot seven times out of ten. Flushed with satisfaction, I smile at Soteli Ma without thinking. Her expression darkens, and I find myself in the cellar again. It is some time before I realize that she hadn't answered my question.

Soteli Ma's hut truly is at the edge of the kingdom— far from civilization, far, even, from roads that could take us to civilization. Passersby are rare—so much so that when a band of troubadours passes in front of the hut, I mistake their chatter for birdsong.

I am too excited to see them to feel ashamed of my ragged appearance. Six months ago, these men would have sung and danced for me in the palace hall. They would have strewn petals at my feet and called me Light-of-the-World. Now we drink from the same tin cup at Soteli Ma's cooking fire. In their eyes, I am no different from her.

Soteli Ma bids the travelers welcome, but I can tell she is not happy. I beg for news of the court and hear, at last, of the rise of the *rakshasa*s. Sightings are now a daily occurrence. Threats issue from the mouths of the possessed, warning of the coming destruction. What we once viewed as folklore has become strategy. Sages read the story of Rustam and the Demon from the *Shah-nama* in the palace library, gleaning what facts they can. Every performance, every recitation of the story of Rama and Ravana is analyzed as military intelligence. The people pray to God to send them an army of fire. The winter crops founder in the fields. And still the djinns have not returned.

"There are signs," the leader says, as the travelers rise

to leave. "They say you can always tell a *deo* by its backwards feet; its fiery eyes and lolling tongue."

I rise with them. For a moment, I consider following. I could tell them who I am—tell them of my torment at the hands of my stepmother—a stranger, who wed my father for no reason I can figure, a witch who cares for nothing so much as ridding me of every last trace of delicacy and nobility I possess.

Soteli Ma watches the troubadours as they crest the hill. "They are fools," she says.

"At least we know what to watch for—backwards feet, fiery eyes."

Soteli Ma grabs my arm and looks me right in the eye. "You'll see what they want you to see. A cousin. A lover. Your heart's desire. They kill as easily by trickery as by might."

I stare at Soteli Ma, dumbstruck, as she retrieves the tin cup from the ground. It may be the longest conversation we have ever had. And it is the only time she has ever touched me without violence.

With the failure of the Rabi harvest, Soteli Ma no longer goes to market. Sometimes she joins me in foraging, digging up wild tubers, shooting fat quails with a makeshift slingshot.

But today I am alone in the woods. I am collecting beechnuts high in the canopy of a tree when the sky goes dark. Deep black. Not like dusk, or the gradual covering of the sun by another heavenly body. It is immediate, like canvas thrown over my head. Like the cellar door slamming shut.

I quiet my breath. I listen. The birds have gone silent. All life in the forest has gone silent, uncertain, waiting.

I look skyward; there are no stars, no moon. This is no ordinary night. A singular thought comes into my mind: Soteli Ma will know what to do.

I grab hold of the branch I am perched on, and stretch a foot down to the tree limb below. I climb down branch after branch. Insects dash out from under my feet, in that preternatural way they have of knowing without seeing. I am struck by how like them I have become.

When I reach the ground, it is familiar. My feet follow the path, silent, deliberate. The stream babbles to the west of me. I reach a hillock and head east, crossing the tree line. The hut can be no more than 500 feet away, but I cannot see it. Soteli Ma has lit neither candle nor oil lamp. I can smell the smoke from our cooking fire, but the flames have been snuffed out.

I walk in the direction of the hut, my hand outstretched. The door opens with a swoosh and Soteli Ma pulls me inside.

"What's happening?" I ask.

"They have cast their nets across the sky," she says.

I open my mouth to speak, but she places a finger on my lips. She is pushing me down to the cellar. To my surprise, she follows. I can hear her scooping handfuls of soil from the rancid ground. She rubs the slime on my arms, legs, my face and hair, then goes still.

I quiet my breath. Close my eyes, my mouth. I wait.

Something is coming. A disturbance in the stale air, taking shape. It presses against me. Sniffs.

I quiet the beat of my heart.

A tongue fat as entrails drags over my face. I don't flinch. I can stand like this for hours if I have to.

When the creature leaves, I can feel it—a change in the pressure, like an indrawn breath—like a lid pried open. I follow Soteli Ma out of the cellar.

"We are leaving," she says.

The hills in the distance are burning. It gives off a sliver of light, a false dawn. We set off into the forest, running. It is another first: I am the one in pursuit.

I follow the sound of Soteli Ma's footsteps on the pine-needled path. A fugitive hope steals into my heart as I run. I have faith in the sureness of my feet.

After several hours, we stop. In mute agreement, we gather tree nuts, wild carrots. We eat. I am bursting with questions. Emboldened by the run, I turn to Soteli Ma.

"Why did you marry my father?" I ask. "Did you love him?"

Soteli Ma stops chewing.

"No," she says.

"Then why?"

She is quiet for a long time.

"It was in payment of a debt," she says.

We settle onto a bed of ferns and sleep. I dream of my lady mother. She is walking through the chambers of the palace, closing and locking the door of each room as she goes. The Women's Quarters. Bath. The Hall of Private Attendance. She pulls the carpets off the walls of the Grand Pavilion. In the courtyard, the water in the fountain sputters and drops. She turns and waves to me. The palace is getting smaller and smaller. I can see the gardens. The royal menagerie. The hunting grounds. The tenant farms. And still, the tiny hand of my lady mother, waving—as if I am the one who is leaving, not her.

The Night is unrelenting. Without the sun, we can no longer reckon the passing of time. I do not know how many weeks we spend wandering, like ruminants, living off the land. I eat only plants and insects, for Soteli Ma refuses to build a fire, and I cannot stomach raw game. We keep our distance from any human settlement. Fires blaze on the horizon. We wait.

In these weeks, Soteli Ma and I achieve a kind of unaccustomed truce. Not a rapprochement—more like the efficiency of common purpose. It is a strange time. If not for the darkness and the faint smell of smoke from the fires in the distance, I could almost believe we were at peace.

I have just eaten a ripe guava—a rare treat after endless meals of bland roots and bitter tree nuts. I allow myself a moment of pleasure, savoring the tart flesh, the gritty texture.

Soteli Ma and I crest a small hill when the smell of smoke and burnt meat assails us. I climb a fig tree and look out over the countryside.

It is a village, smoldering. From the treetops, it looks deserted. The only movement I can see is the flicker of flames, the only sound the faint crackle of fire as it feeds.

I stare at the scene, unblinking. Suddenly I am on the ground, racing past the tree line, toward the flames. I expect Soteli Ma to stop me, but she does not. She stands at the edge of the village. I wander among the bodies, breathless.

They must have gathered around the cooking fire, in twos and threes. Lovers. Families. Children on laps. Babies in arms. I am suddenly angry. Enraged by their stupidity.

"Why didn't they run? Why did they light a fire? Why did they make themselves such a target?"

I am sputtering, I'm so angry.

"Chakoo."

"If they had just—"

"Chakoo!"

I look up at Soteli Ma, startled. Her expression is grim, but calm.

"They clung to each other," she says. "They took comfort in the light. Isn't that what people do?"

I look down at the blackened bodies. Clasping. Fused.

Yes, I think. That is what people do.

But not us.

Soteli Ma turns and heads back to the forest. To darkness. Alone.

And I follow.

We are running again. We run until we have left the smell of burnt flesh far behind us. And then we sleep. I do not know for how long, but it feels like days.

When word of the first *rakshasa* sightings reached the palace, my cousins and I were strangely excited. It was as if we were living in a time of legends. I didn't understand why my father so vehemently dismissed the sightings, why he attempted—without success—to quell the burgeoning stories. Perhaps he thought to avert panic, stockpiling, despair. He needn't have worried. The people of the kingdom met the threat with stoic acceptance. After all, this war, should it arrive, would not be fought by them. Hadn't Ravana and the demon horde of Lanka been driven back by Lord Rama and his monkey warriors? Wouldn't an army of *shayatan* be met by an army of angels? Bystanders, pawns, we would live or we would die; there was nothing we could do, except pray.

As far as we could tell, Beings of Fire were largely indifferent to the troubles of humans; but they were not entirely immune to our flattery, or our fervent pleas for aid. Thus, after weeks of darkness, when the people of the kingdom awoke to find what looked like stars in the sky, we allowed ourselves to hope that our entreaties had been heard—that an army of fire had finally arrived, to beat back the Night.

It is strange to walk in the forest by starlight, if that's what this is. I feel exposed and uneasy. Soteli Ma's profile unnerves me, spare and stern in the unfamiliar glow. The dim outline of the trees, the leaves, even my own hands seem alien, out of place.

We wander the forest, aimless. The air is stale, like a boarded up cave—and tense, like something waiting to happen. It is almost a relief when it does. The sky breaks with a palpable crack, and we run again. Faster, this time, for we know we have been found.

A wave of menace huffs behind me, like the open mouths of a hundred wild dogs. I scramble over rocks, tree roots.

Soteli Ma steers us west, off the path, across the stream. She reaches down and grabs a stick as she runs.

"The eyes," she says. "It will blind them."

I glance over my shoulder mid-stride. The *rakshasa*s have taken the shape of wolves, large as bears. The troubadour was right; their eyes glow red, like fire.

Soteli Ma hurls a stick behind her, and another, striking her target each time. Blinded, the wounded *rakshasa*s fall under the feet of their fellows. I follow Soteli Ma's lead, grabbing sticks and hurling them at my pursuers, rejoicing each time a pair of red eyes goes out.

Soteli Ma does not seem to tire, and she is faultless in her aim. While my volleys grow increasingly wild, hers continue to hit their targets. I do not know how many demons lie blinded, over how many miles, nor how many remain. I focus all my energy on flight.

Above us, the stars grow brighter, bigger, like sparks burning holes in a black curtain. I can see a ravine, unbridged, in the distance. Soteli Ma sees it, too. We will not be able to cross.

"The trees!" she shouts.

Soteli Ma leaps up and grabs the lowest branch of a towering banyan tree, pulling herself up with ease. I make a dash for the same tree, but my foot sinks into a snarl of knotted roots. Thrown off balance, I fall. I scramble to stand, but my foot is wedged tight. Behind me, three—no, four *rakshasa*s approach.

I hear the snap of a branch breaking and a clack as Soteli Ma brings down another demon. I struggle to free my foot. The more I pull, the more it tightens, like a noose.

I reach for the dagger at my calf.

It was not built for use. It barely has an edge. But it is all I have.

The panting of the demons grows closer. I hear another one fall. I slide the blade of the dagger beneath the roots and start cutting.

Two *rakshasa*s remain, not 20 feet away. Soteli Ma strikes another. I focus on the movement of the blade, on the fibers of the root as they begin, slowly, to weaken.

One demon is left. It is larger than the others—rank, teeth like spikes, dripping tar. I watch its approach as I cut. It is so close that when Soteli Ma puts out its eyes with one final volley, the stick rebounds and strikes my cheek.

The *rakshasa* is blind, but it does not fall. It knows I

am near. It sniffs, waves its fat tongue like some prehensile limb. I close my eyes. My mouth. I continue to saw through the root, but silently, with uncanny economy. Finally, the root gives way with the smallest of sighs. The *rakshasa* swings its massive head toward the sound. I raise my hand in the air, and Soteli Ma is pulling me up, into the canopy, to safety.

Minutes pass. I open my eyes. Above us, the holes of light continue to grow. I look down at the ground. The wounded demon flickers and vanishes, and cool, clean air rushes into the forest, rousing the leaves.

I am alive. I am also no longer afraid. I turn to Soteli Ma.

"How did you know what to do?" I ask. "How do you know these things? Why did my father want to marry you? *Who are you*?"

Soteli Ma looks up at the sky, the patches of Night diminishing.

"I will tell you a story," she says.

Once upon a time, a king was riding in the royal hunting grounds when he came upon a fawn, caught in a poacher's snare. The king freed the poor animal and carried it back to the royal menagerie, that it could heal in safety and comfort. Time passed, and the fawn recovered. When the king released it in the royal forest, it transformed into a human woman, revealing herself as a *rakshasi*. Filled with gratitude, the *rakshasi* warned the king of a coming calamity—a spirit battle not seen in this world for centuries.

"They will strike at the court," she warned. "First you. Then your daughter. Holy men. Nobles. Peasants. They delight in killing humans, as a provocation to the Gods."

"Can you stop this war from coming?" the king asked.

"No."

"Can you save my kingdom?"

"No."

"Can you save my daughter?"

The *rakshasi* hesitated.

"*Can you save my daughter?*" the king pressed.

"Perhaps."

I want to kill her.

I want to cut off her head.

Not because she is one of them, but because she contrived to save me, while the world burned.

I hear a rustle in the ferns below us. A woodsman, bearing an axe, bursts through the thicket.

"Come out, dear ladies!" he calls. "The demons are vanquished! The war is won."

My heart's desire! I will denounce Soteli Ma, and he will cut her down.

From the corner of my eye, I see Soteli Ma make an almost imperceptible shake of her head. I hesitate.

Once more, I quiet my breath. The branch sways, as if to crack. I become small, light, part of the tree. I close my mouth, my eyes, letting nothing out nor in.

When I open them again, the last of the demon Night slips from the sky. The woodsman flickers, like sun through a cloud, and is gone.

All the fight goes out of me. Without a word, Soteli Ma and I drop to the ground. We push through the thicket, past the tree line and into the open countryside. Into the light. It is dazzling. Disorienting.

"Why don't you go back to your own kind?" I ask at last. "You've settled your debt to my father."

Soteli Ma pauses, an unfamiliar uncertainty in her eyes.

"I am no longer one kind or another," she says.

It is a long walk back to Soteli Ma's hut, made longer by the tumult in my mind.

The kingdom is rebuilding. Soon market days resume, and Soteli Ma does not protest when I accompany her. I gather what news I can of the court. My cousin Raihan Sultan Beg has taken the throne. He will be a good king, I think. But I feel strangely detached.

One summer morning, a courtier rides up, handsome, on a royal steed. I have just come back from the stream, a large clay jar of water balanced on my head.

"I beg your pardon, good miss," the courtier says. "I am looking for word of the Princess Rania Shah Sultan Begum. She may have passed through these parts, before the war."

I take in the fine silk crest of his waistcoat, the rings of gold and topaz on his fingers. His fair, scrubbed face. The kindness in his eyes.

"There are no princesses here," I say, lifting the jar of water from my head and placing it at my bare feet.

The courtier bows.

"May I know your good name?" he says.

I look over at the forest—at Soteli Ma gathering

firewood, her back bent, her black hair a tangle on her shoulders.

I give the courtier a small bow in return.

"My name is Chakoo," I say.

Laura Ring is an anthropologist and academic librarian living in Chicago. She is the author of *Zenana: Everyday Peace in a Karachi Apartment Building* (Indiana University Press 2006).

Wolfsbane

C.H. Spalding

The Romans were gone, Arthur was dead, and the Wolf was coming.

Portius paused in the shadows of the last line of trees to catch his breath. The Wolf's army had smashed the mud and straw huts across the river, and when he'd left, the army had been both burning and tearing apart the wooden palisades by the ford. They were headed for the old Roman fort on the hill. The curl of smoke on the horizon hopefully meant that it was not deserted.

He set off again, forcing his aching legs and seared lungs to finish the long climb. He'd been running since daybreak; the sun was a little past its zenith. With looting and pillaging, the army was probably a day behind him. Probably.

As he neared the stone walls more signs of life became obvious. Outside fire pits roasted sides of beef and whole hogs, while a steady stream of people went in and out of the front doors. He was relieved to see that there were actually guards at the doors, a mismatch of Briton and Saxon weaponry and discarded Roman armor.

He slowed a little as he neared. His darker skin and hair already made him an object of distrust even when he didn't approach like a rabid dog. He met the gaze of the first guard, a middle aged man with graying hair and beard, and spoke his message without stuttering.

"I need to speak with your leader. The Wolf is coming."

The guards exchanged glances.

"He'd better be seeing the Red, then," a younger guard interjected, and the graying man nodded.

"I'll need your weapon."

The woodcutter's axe would be all but useless against the army that was coming. Portius surrendered it silently, then submitted to a quick but thorough search. At length the older guard nodded his permission.

"How shall I announce you?" the younger guard asked. He looked barely fourteen, freckled and blond, and Portius grimaced. Seventeen had never felt so old.

"Portius, from the east, Theoford." The Saxons ruled that area now, and they were supposed to stop pushing the islanders west. But the Wolf kept coming. The Wolf wanted more.

The boy only nodded, and led him inside. There were Briton-made hangings on the walls and fur rugs by the fire, with rushes elsewhere to dull the cold from the stone. A slight figure stood backlit by the fire, turning towards them as they entered.

"Yes, Hamish?"

"It's Portius, from East Engle way. He's asked to speak with you, says the Wolf is coming."

There was rueful amusement in the voice that answered. "We knew that, I think. Still, news is always welcome. Come in and be welcome, Portius." The figure stepped back, so that firelight gleamed off a face that was barely older than the guard's ... and female. "I am Rovena, called the Red."

Hamish hesitated. "Should I stay?"

Rovena smiled. "No, go ask Alden to bring up some warmed wine and a bit of food. My guest has come some distance from the look of him."

Portius came in hesitantly. "Lady Rovena ... are you the widow of the Lord here?"

"Daughter." She sat, and gestured him to the chair beside her. "If I were only a widow, we'd none of us be having this trouble." She cocked her head, smiling as if reading his confusion. "My father married me to the Wolf two months back to secure a peace. After he sacked several more of our villages, I decided he was wanting as a husband and left him. If I could have left him in pieces, believe me, I would have."

"He let you leave?" Portius realized that he was gaping and closed his mouth.

"He did not." Rovena met his eyes frankly, as West Island women tended to do. "He thought that two guards were enough to keep a Briton woman in line. He was ... mistaken." Her hand closed in a way that made him not want to ask about the fate of the guards. "So, you bring news of my husband?"

Portius shook himself, then tersely described the fate of the huts and the palisades. "The stone here won't burn. With the cisterns, you'll have water in plenty, and I see you are gathering in food. Your best chance—your only chance—is to outwait him."

Rovena nodded an acknowledgement, then gestured to a side doorway where a serving man waited. "I'll show you the cisterns after you've eaten. You've earned a meal with your warning."

The cisterns had been allowed to fall in disrepair, but should be easy to fix. Portius went over them with growing excitement. "I can improve on them for you. With these, water won't be a problem."

Rovena was watching him, an odd expression on her face. "You are a builder, then?"

"An architect. Or I would be, if I could. I like working with wood and stone." He grimaced. "I'm a bastard, and unacknowledged. The only place for me in Roman society would be as a soldier ... and war isn't my strong suit."

She was kind enough not to laugh at the obviousness of that. He was barely taller than her, and would give even odds that she was stronger. Instead she nodded again, stared out over the hills, and abruptly spoke.

"We don't have enough food."

She turned back to look at him, and he could see the fatalistic calm in her eyes. "Either we turn out people, and don't have enough to keep the invaders away, or we all starve. I was thinking poison might be kinder. I wouldn't surrender a dog to that bastard."

"Oh." Portius leaned back against the wall, staring blankly at the tile that turned it into a pool when the gutters were closed off. "I hadn't thought beyond getting here."

Rovena shook her head. "You'll want to keep going. We'll likely delay them a few weeks, but no one in this land will be safe until the Wolf is dead. I'd surrender myself to him, but there's no way he'd let me near him with weapons, especially after … well." She cleared her throat. "I do appreciate the warning, though."

His brain was buzzing, equations and possibilities shoving at one another to be heard. "We need to trick him."

"Trick him? How? He's the Wolf. He has an army." Rovena smiled sadly. "Kindness isn't much of an asset in this world."

"I wasn't thinking of being kind." Portius felt his face twist into a crooked smile. "We're smarter than he is. That will be enough."

Four hours later the whole Clan saw Portius tossed out on his ear as their Mistress called him a dirty Roman spy, a coward, and a fool. Hamish tossed his axe after him, a look of reluctant pity on his face, while Portius raised his fist and swore the Red would be sorry.

He stomped down the lengthy hill until he was out of sight of the Fort then gathered his strength and his courage for the next part. When he encountered the scouts for the Wolf's army on the road, he marched up to them, head held high.

"Bring me to the Wolf," he said. "Tell him I'm going to deliver his shrew of a wife to him and her hall beside."

The Wolf was a big man, tall and broad with an iron gray beard and a hooked nose that reminded Portius more of eagle than wolf. He did not look like an idiot, or someone who suffered fools gladly. "Is this the boy who will give me the Red?"

Portius was thrust forward. "Yes." He tried to stand up tall, to be angry and believable. "Rovena promised my family they could seek shelter at her fort. When I got there, she had turned them out. I have no idea where they are now."

"Why should I care about this?" growled the Wolf, his dark gray eyes growing unfocused … and perhaps angry, impatient.

"Because Rovena lied to my family," Portius claimed, making a fist. "She's not short on food. She has months of it stocked away, all manner of grains, even livestock." He smiled a predatory smile, lowering his voice. "But she squats in a Roman fort, Caer Caradoc. My grandfather was a Roman. I know how to crack her fort."

The approaches to Caer Caradoc were not inviting. On one side it was very steep, and on the rest was a gentler, but wide-open expanse. All trees on these approaches had been chopped down. The Caradoc defenders would have ample time to rain down stones and arrows as the Wolf's men climbed toward them.

"Bah, we can starve them out. There's no way any supplies could be weaseled in to her." The Wolf had actually been given pause.

"My lord, she expects you to do that," Portius said earnestly. "A battering ram also would be accounted for. The Red's fort is set up to defend against attackers at her doors. I can lead you up and over, to come in from the top rather than trying to get through the bottom."

The Wolf grunted. After a long pause he motioned to several of his men. "Make me ladders." He turned to Portius, scowling. "You're going to lead this attack, boy, and if you've led me wrong I'll crush your skull with my own two hands."

Portius nodded, trying to look calm. "I'd expect no less."

By the time the ladders were finished night was falling. The Wolf directed his men to darken their faces and arms with mud or pitch and paced until darkness had settled. There was no moon, and light clouds obscured the stars. A few lights were visible from the Fort itself, but the way was dark.

"The more of your men we can get onto the roof before they know we're there, the fewer casualties we'll take," Portius informed the Wolf as they started the surprisingly quiet assent.

The Wolf grunted. "Teach your grandmother to card wool, boy. I've been a soldier since before you were born."

Portius ducked his head and focused on making it up the steep grade. There was no cry from the Fort, no sign that they had been spotted, and the first ladder had no more been lifted against the wall then the Wolf was lifting him bodily onto it. Portius climbed rapidly, aware of the Wolf climbing a breath behind.

There was enough room on the roof for a good hundred of the Wolf's men without crowding. Damp rushes on the roof muffled their steps, and Portius whispered as he directed the Wolf to the center.

"See, the chimney is cool. It's Roman build, big enough for a bear to fit through. This will take us into the kitchens, which are in the center of the Fort. We'll be among them before we even know they're there."

The Wolf grunted. "I'll be right behind you. Let's make sure you don't get too far ahead." He tied a rope around him, just below Portius's armpits, and yanked on it once for emphasis.

The chimney was slick, and the rope helped slow Portius as he descended. He could hear but not see the Wolf descending above him. It was dark below, and he had to guess his position until he came to the narrower section before the fireplace opened. At last his feet reached the bottom, and he jerked twice on the rope.

Rovena was standing beside the fireplace, a single candle just enough to show the smile on her face, the blade in her hand. The blade struck out, severing the rope, and then she looked up into the darkness above. A sudden thump showed when the Wolf reached the narrow part—the only part of the chimney where a bear, or a Wolf, could not pass.

Curses were coming down as Rovena lit a torch from the candle and touched it to the oil and twine that ran up the chimney and beneath the oil soaked rushes above. The burst of flame illuminated her face, cheerful as she listened to the screams of her former husband and of his men above.

"I swear I will never underestimate a Briton woman," Portius breathed, and she laughed.

"And I'll swear to never underestimate a part-Roman architect. How long do you think it will take to clean the cisterns, after?"

"A few good rains will do it." They listened to the sounds of chaos above, as ladders toppled beneath the frantic men trying to descend them. "We'll need to clean the chimney, after it cools."

Rovena nodded, building up the fire in the chimney to finish what they had started. "Welcome to Caer Caradoc, Portius. Health to our friends, death to our enemies, and farewell to the Wolf."

C. H. Spalding has been writing short stories since the 1980s or before. Only claim to fame: having dinner with Anne McCaffrey in 1992, then nervously pushing her in a wheelchair around the Atlanta airport to get her to her flight. She wanted to take the escalator at one point. Oh God, the terror.

The River's Blessing
Ameria Lewis

Once upon a time, in a land far away, there was a pretty village beside a chuckling little river. The river was known for its clarity and sweetness and its occasionally magical healing properties. The villagers were very proud of their river, and that their king and queen had chosen the village to be their summer home. During those long, warm months each year it was common to see young princes and princesses riding through the fields and forests, their lively voices carried gaily on the air.

Legend had it that the little river had been blessed by a fairy who lived at its source. As long as no one lived further upstream than the little village, the water would continue to be sweet and pure and occasionally healing. Legend also told that once, the river always healed, but when word spread the village had been mobbed, the river sullied, and the waters nearly drained full away. That was when the fairy came and cleared the river, returned the water, and dammed the magic away so that it could only be used with her permission.

No one knew where the fairy lived. Many had sought her. Very few had found her, and those few had long since gone to their rest. The legends continued and grew in the telling, but the river remained pure and protected.

One day, an older man with three children moved to the village. He was a sophisticated man, accustomed to living in the King's City. He lived in a fine house with his daughters and his son, with a grand garden and many servants. He hosted teas and balls and invited everyone in the village. It did not take long for Lord Gavin to become as beloved as the king and his family in the little village.

His daughters were shy young ladies, dressed in pretty dresses and given everything they wanted. They moved with delicacy and grace, and seemed innocent and kind. They served tea to the village children and shared their satin ribbons. They taught the dance steps to the girls and blushed when the young men smiled at them.

His son, the eldest of his children, was not expected to have such fine sensibilities. He was rambunctious and adventuresome. He played pranks on his sisters, spent his days riding through the countryside and his nights carousing in the local tavern. He was popular with the other young men of the village and if the lasses sighed over him more than the other lads, well, where was the harm? Young Lord William had a bright future as the sole heir to his father's fortune.

A few weeks after their arrival in the village, a young woman considered well past the proper age to marry, but certainly far from her thirtieth year, caught Lord Gavin's eye. Alyssa was not the most beautiful woman in the village, being plump of form and of common coloring. Her skin was olive and in the summer quite brown. Her hair was also brown, with no spark of red or glint of gold. Her brown eyes were dark and soft and were, without doubt, her finest feature. She dressed neatly in colors that were pretty but never in the latest fashion. She lived with her eldest brother and tended his children. In public she was often in the background, carrying a toddler or holding the hand of a small child.

How she and Lord Gavin became acquainted no one knew. He was considerably older than she. She stayed home with the children while her brother and his wife enjoyed Lord Gavin's balls and teas. It came as a surprise to the whole village when Lord Gavin drove up to Miss Alyssa's house and then drove away again with her at his side. Their first stop was the village magistrate where they filed their intention to wed in two weeks. Their second was his home, where he informed his children that they would soon have a new mother.

Young Lord William was not pleased and extended his new mother-to-be no welcome. She was of child-bearing years, and William saw his inheritance threatened with potential new brothers. His sisters were reserved, but said all that was proper and expected, took Miss Alyssa's hand and kissed her cheek. When dismissed, they left the room quietly with Miss Alyssa no wiser to their feelings.

The two weeks before the wedding passed swiftly as the girls helped with the planning. Ginnia, the elder girl, showed Alyssa how to arrange seating and plan menus. Alyssa discovered that Ginnia enjoyed working in the kitchen when her father was not around. Heather, the younger girl, was skilled with floral arrangements and confided in Alyssa a few secrets of the art that made the task simple. Heather, Alyssa found, preferred being outside and working in a garden, but she always kept a hat on and wore protective gloves so her complexion and hands did not betray her pastime.

Alyssa felt a fondness for the girls grow in her heart, but she could not understand the distance they kept from her, despite their kindness and confidences. They would not laugh with her and seldom smiled, but their eyes watched her with cautious warmth. However, Alyssa trusted that the love she had found with their father would warm their hearts in time and they would become a family in truth.

Young Lord William was a problem, openly snubbing her in the streets of the little village. As the wedding day approached, Alyssa feared that he would refuse to attend the wedding at all. It would shame the family and set her marriage off to a very bad start. She voiced her doubts to Lord Gavin, only to be reassured.

"It is his way, my dear. Do not fret," Gavin assured her warmly, drawing her hand through the crook of his arm as he walked in his garden with her one fine May morning. "He is young and foolish. He fears that you will give me sons and displace him."

Alyssa blushed even as she looked away and smiled. "I would like to give you a son, my love, but I will have him when I wear your ring."

"And more still, is my hope," Lord Gavin chuckled.

"At least one babe with your pretty eyes, promise me, my darling."

"What is meant to be will be," was all Alyssa would say, refusing to be lured into making promises that she did not know if she could keep. "I would not come between you and your children."

Lord Gavin's chin lifted and his eyes narrowed. "I give my children everything they desire. They will give me this. The girls have not made it difficult for you, I trust?"

"No, of course not," Alyssa assured him. "They have been very kind."

"As they should be," Gavin nodded. "They know better than to be anything else."

Alyssa's brows wrinkled as she looked at Gavin in puzzlement. What an odd thing to say!

"Stop that now, my darling," Lord Gavin chided, smoothing a finger over the creased skin between her brows. "You'll wrinkle your skin if you frown so. Come see the arbor the gardener has completed for the ceremony. You will be pleased."

Alyssa forgot her puzzlement and went where Lord Gavin led her. She had little time to wonder or worry as her wedding day approached. The whole village was excited for their resident 'old maid.'

The wedding day dawned with cloudy sky and the rumbling of thunder. Alyssa was not dismayed. She arrived at Lord Gavin's home early and when the girls voiced their apologies over the turn in the weather, Alyssa reassured them.

"Oh, my dears, it doesn't matter!" she exclaimed, linking her arms through theirs and leading them up the stairs to the rooms that would become her very own that day. "Sun or shower, I love your father and today we will be wed. If it rains, we'll do it inside." She smiled brightly. "But it will not rain. Within two hours, I promise you, the sky will be blue again."

Sending the girls off to get ready for the wedding, Alyssa entered her own room and locked her door. With a secret smile, she crossed the room and looked out the window, up into the grey and threatening clouds. "There is farmland nearby that needs your rain much more than the village does. Won't you move just a bit and rain there instead?" she asked the cloud. The cloud gave no response, but who would expect that it would? Alyssa turned away from the window and headed for her waiting bath, humming a happy song as she went.

When all was ready and the guests began arriving—

the whole village had been invited, of course!—there were still clouds in the sky, but off to the west, over the grain fields. The rain came down thick and heavy, but the village remained dry with a blue sky above. When the girls commented on how lucky it was, Alyssa laughed and said that sometimes all it took was asking politely.

It was a beautiful and simple wedding. Alyssa glowed as she looked at her new husband and no one in the village could deny that for their spinster, it was love. They still couldn't figure out what a handsome, older, prosperous man like Lord Gavin could see in Alyssa, but since his eyes stayed on her and he smiled for her, they assumed it was love, as well.

The household settled into a new routine, and for a while there was a brightness in the big house that hadn't been there before. Alyssa often sang at whatever task she was about, and she found many tasks for herself. At first Lord Gavin chided her gently for doing the servants' jobs and Alyssa had to admit that if she did their jobs, then they would have nothing to do. She turned her attention to the needs of the villagers, arriving in the village with a basket over her arm and knocking on the doors of the poorest residents. Sometimes Ginnia and Heather accompanied her. Sometimes they did not. Eventually a pattern developed: if Lord Gavin were home, they stayed home. If he were away, they accompanied Alyssa.

After a year, Alyssa gave Lord Gavin the joyous news that she was with child. Her heart was full: a husband to love, a child to come, and three children already there and cherished in her heart—even William with his simmering resentment. Vain and selfish he may be, but Alyssa had seen him stop his horse in the middle of the road and pull the baker's boy up with him when the lad was walking with a limp. She had seen him help an elderly widow carry her market goods inside then stop long enough to rehang a fallen shutter. She had watched him tease his sisters into blushes then spend time dancing with them so their steps would be perfect at the frequent balls their father hosted.

Yes, William might dislike her, but she loved him. Golden-haired Ginnia might be reserved, but she was kind and thoughtful. Heather, with her darker blonde hair and green eyes might be elusive, but she was sweet and impulsive and easily contented. Alyssa knew the girls would welcome another child to the family, and hoped William's ire would recede when the child arrived.

As her pregnancy progressed, Lord Gavin spent more

time at home. Although she felt healthy and strong, Lord Gavin forbade her to continue her visits in the village as they were too taxing on her strength. Alyssa protested, but Lord Gavin could not be swayed and her arguments brought a dark light to his eyes. Alyssa subsided, confused by this new facet in her beloved husband. He had encouraged her visits before. Why change now?

One by one, each of the duties she'd created for herself were taken away, always with the explanation that it wasn't good for the baby. By the time she entered her last month, Alyssa could do nothing but sit in the garden or the drawing room and play at needlework, a skill she had never fully mastered. She assured herself that once the babe came things would return to normal. But she wondered and worried. Her husband did not seem the same man she had married.

The day finally came and Alyssa labored long to deliver her child. Lord Gavin waited outside the door with his daughters standing quietly at his side. Finally the wail of a newborn came from the room and Lord Gavin threw open the doors. He strode inside and went straight to the nurse.

"Well?" he demanded impatiently without glancing at the weary Alyssa.

"You have another beautiful daughter, Lord Gavin," the midwife said happily, busy washing the child in a basin of warm water.

"Another worthless daughter?" Lord Gavin demanded, spinning to stride towards the bed. His hand swung down and the sound of the slap echoed into the hall.

"Father!" Heather cried, darting between Alyssa and Lord Gavin's hand as it swung again. She cried out as the blow took her instead.

"Out of my way, brat!" Gavin growled, grabbing Heather's arm and throwing her across the room. He slapped Alyssa again. "You were supposed to give me a son, not another blasted girl!"

"Heather?" Ginnia said softly, hesitating in the doorway, her wide eyes on her sister's crumpled and unmoving form. "Heather!"

Lord Gavin barely glanced at his fallen daughter as he brushed past the one still standing. Alyssa watched him leave with tears falling down her red-stained cheeks. He had struck her. He had struck Heather, who had only sought to protect her. Who was this man in her husband's body? Where was the kindness, the gentleness?

Ginnia darted for Heather and the village woman quietly folded a soft blanket around the newborn. As Ginnia straightened Heather's limbs and ran her hands around them, the midwife laid the baby in Alyssa's arms. The baby girl had dark hair like Alyssa, and a complexion like hers as well. Alyssa was torn between nursing the newborn and going to Heather's side. She started to rise, but the midwife pushed her back down.

"You're job's not done yet, child," she said sympathetically. "Nurse your babe. I'll tend to Miss Heather and Miss Ginnia." She went to the two girls, pausing only to use the bell pull to call a footman.

While her daughter nursed hungrily at her breast, Alyssa watched anxiously as the footman carefully lifted Heather and carried her out of the door. "I'll be there as soon as I can get up, Ginnia," she promised the older daughter.

The girl paused at the doorway but barely turned her head to answer. "No, Stepmother. It would only anger him more, and now that you've had the baby …." Ginnia's shoulders shifted in the hint of a shrug. A sob caught in her throat. "There's a spot on Heather's head that's soft. Coming won't fix that, but it might give you a soft head, too."

Alyssa caught her breath and stared at the empty

doorway. She looked down at her daughter and felt a seed of fear grow in her heart. She knew what she had to do. There really was no choice.

For three days she rested and healed and nursed baby Amber. For three days, she received hourly updates on Heather's unchanging condition. At the end of three days, she could delay no longer. She waited until Lord Gavin had left the house then ordered a wagon hitched, Heather bundled up and laid inside. She and Ginnia packed the girls' bags and joined Heather in the wagon. They sat quietly while the coachman drove them to her brother's home, taking a circular route so their destination was not initially obvious.

Alyssa left the girls there and promised to return. Her brother promised to take care of them until that time and, without knowing why it was necessary, to hide them from their father. Worried, he and his wife watched as Alyssa packed a basket and covered it with a pretty cloth. Alyssa kissed her infant daughter and brushed the hair from Ginnia's forehead. She bent over Heather and kissed her, too, and then walked out the door without a backward look.

There are legends and legends, and all have a seed of truth to them. Alyssa knew this and went searching for the only one who could save Heather, prepared to pay the price. She found the bank of the pure, sweet river and followed it upstream. She walked all day, determined to waste no more time. Heather had so little left. The girl's life had been fading slowly over the past three days. She didn't have two more.

Dusk came, and still Alyssa walked. The light of the moon and the stars guided her feet and she followed the path they laid. She was stumbling with exhaustion when a musical voice called to her.

"Cease your steps and take your ease, young mother. You have walked this long way, stopping for no rest. You have found what you seek. Speak why you have sought me."

Alyssa swayed in the moonlight, her tired mind struggling with the thought that she could stop moving.

"I-I have come with a gift to ask a boon, magical one," she finally said, peering around the darkened forest.

"Ah, a bribe for a boon," the fairy said, stepping out into the moonlight. Her gown was gossamer fine and lay over her form like a dream. Dragonfly wings flickered at her back, reflecting moonlight in glittering shimmers.

"No, my lady, no bribe. The gift is yours whether

or not you grant the boon." Alyssa swayed again, then sank slowly to her knees. She was so tired.

"Hmm." The fairy lifted her hand and the basket floated towards her. When she removed the checked cloth, she smiled in delight. "Why, tis lovely!" She lifted out the framed watercolor picture of Alyssa's favorite bend in the little river, brightly colored with springtime flowers, a blue sky overhead. Beneath the painting was a loaf of bread, a wheel of cheese, and a selection of vegetables from the garden. "I will hear the boon you ask of me."

Alyssa cried silent tears. "Please, Lady Fairy, please. My daughter is injured, dying. Only with your blessing will the waters of the river heal her."

The fairy's delight vanished. She returned the painting to the basket and stepped lightly down the bank. She set the basket beside Alyssa and touched her tears with a gentle fingertip.

"You know magic, young mother. It has a price that must be paid. If a death is coming, it cannot be averted. I will not choose another to take her place so she may live." The fairy's heart-shaped face was sad, but resolved. "Take your gift and return home to say your goodbyes. I am sorry."

"Please." Alyssa grabbed the fairy's hand, desperation quickening her voice. "Please, I'm not asking you to choose another. I offer myself instead! I will take her death if you will but let her live!"

The river fairy tilted her head and looked puzzled. "She is not the child of your body, and you have just borne one that is. You would leave the little one?"

Alyssa blinked back a new wave of tears. "Not happily, but I know Ginnia and Heather will raise their sister well. My brother will hide them from their father until they can be moved to a more distant village. We have a cousin, far away. He will give them a home."

The fairy was not content with this answer. "What is the girl to you, that you trade your life for hers?"

Alyssa shook her head. "She is my daughter, of course, and I love her."

The fairy lifted her head and looked straight towards the road, which came near the river at this point. A horseman paused, his horse rearing a little at the sudden pull on the reins. The fairy and Alyssa had been hidden from his sight until the fairy willed it otherwise.

"Do you hear this, young Lord William? The woman you have despised and scorned this past score of months trades her life for your sister Heather, leaving her own child behind. She will hide your sisters away from your father's anger. What say you?"

William slowly swung out of his saddle and stepped down to the riverbank.

"I am sorry," he told Alyssa humbly. "I was jealous and selfish; I thought you married my father for his money. I see now that you did not." He looked at the fairy. "Take my life instead. She deserves to have her daughter, and she'll take care of my sisters."

The fairy stepped back and shook her head. "Most often the price for a healing is refused. 'Tis seldom indeed the price is agreed to by one, and never by two. Very well, I'll grant the token for the healing, but know this: I cannot say who will pay the price. Magic is willful and has its own way. You know this, young mother, and you respect it. You have but touched the edges of what can be done, and have ventured no further than was safe. Magic approves this respect."

The fairy held out a perfect pink rosebud. "Place this bloom in the bucket of water you draw from the river. Let it rest there until the flower unfurls from its sleep. Have young Heather drink one cup of the water, and pour the rest into a basin. Allow her head to rest almost completely submerged in the water. By morning she will be well, and the price will be paid."

Alyssa gently lifted the rose from the fairy's palm and cupped it in her hands. The fairy tried to hand back the basket but Alyssa refused to take it.

"A gift is a gift," she insisted.

"Come, Aly—Stepmother," William said gently, helping her up the bank to his horse. "We'll get back to the village faster," he added gruffly as he helped her mount behind him. "Hold tight; we'll be going fast."

Alyssa pressed her cheek to William's back and held tight while the gelding launched himself into a ground-devouring canter. If both William's back and his cheeks became wet, neither mentioned it. The distance it had taken Alyssa so many hours to walk flashed by. As they neared the village again William turned his horse off the road to ride through the woods.

"Where are the girls now?" William asked quietly as he guided the horse through a stand of trees.

"At my brother's," Alyssa murmured, aching and stiff.

"Hold on, Stepmother," William said, leaning forward and urging the horse into a fast trot.

Young Lord William's many rides through the countryside had given him a thorough knowledge of how to get to and from anywhere. He used the knowledge now to quickly and covertly reach her brother's house, with only a brief pause at the riverbank to draw the bucket of water. Alyssa dropped the pink rose into the water so it could work the magic needed while they finished their ride.

They arrived in full dark. Only one dim light burned in hope of guiding her home. William helped Alyssa down from his horse, taking the bucket of magical river water from her and carrying it to the door. It opened before they reached it. Ginnia's young face was wan and tired, dark circles bruising the skin beneath her weary green eyes.

Ginnia's eyes widened and the slump vanished from her shoulders.

"Stepmother, you are back!" she exclaimed, throwing the door open and taking a hasty step towards Alyssa before coming to an abrupt halt, her relief dimming just as quickly. "You did not find the fairy."

Alyssa stepped up to her, closing the distance that fear—fear Alyssa now understood—would not allow the girl to cross. She laid her hand gently on Ginnia's cheek.

"I found her," she said gently. "I have it. Come; we must hurry!"

Tears shimmered in Ginnia's eyes, and she opened the door wide. William preceded them inside with the precious bucket, following Alyssa's murmured directions to the room where Heather lay senseless. Her hair was spread neatly over the pillow, its golden glory hidden in the dim candlelight.

"Quickly," Alyssa whispered, reaching for the empty cup on the bedside table. She dipped up the water and settled on the side of the bed. She paused and looked around. "The babe?" One last time she wanted to hold her daughter, let her feel all the love she bore her.

"Here." Ginnia bent over a cradle tucked in the corner of the room and lifted the warm little bundle that slept within. She handed her half-sister to her stepmother and stepped back, watching sadly as Alyssa kissed the soft skin of the baby's forehead.

"Now," Alyssa said. "Lift Heather's head, William. Caress her throat, Ginnia, so she will swallow as I pour the water into her mouth." Together the three accomplished the task, with little spillage, until the cup was empty.

William poured the remaining water into the basin, the pink rose floating serenely on the surface. Ginnia arranged her sister so that her head rested over the side of bed and Alyssa placed a low stool beside it. With the basin on the stool, Heather's head rested completely within the water, only her pale, heart-shaped face visible above it.

The three settled to wait. Alyssa sat in a chair, her babe in one arm and her hand holding Heather's. William leaned against the wall by the window, his face dark and brooding. Ginnia sat on the bed beside Heather, holding her other hand and humming. The long hours of the night passed slowly, quietly, disturbed only by Amber's whimpered pleas for feeding or changing.

Dawn seeped through the world and at last Heather gave a long sigh and opened her eyes.

Tears of joy spilled from Alyssa's eyes. "Oh, darling! William, she's awake!"

Ginnia gave a glad cry and bent to kiss her sister's cheek, mindful of whatever injuries she might still have. Even as William jumped to the bedside and Heather struggled against their arms to sit up, Alyssa's joy dimmed. It was dawn. Heather was healed. It was time.

Alyssa rose to her feet, her movement distracting William. He looked up at her;his smile faded and he too rose. Alyssa bent and kissed Ginnia's forehead, and then Heather's. She placed sleeping Amber in Ginnia's arms.

"Care for her and love her, as I love all of you," she said gently, touching Heather's hair. "My beautiful, wonderful children. You will be safe, and never have cause to fear again. I promise you."

"It's time?" William asked somberly.

"It's time." Alyssa accepted the arm that William extended to her and together they walked from the room. "I would like to see the sunrise."

"It is a beautiful time of day," young Lord William agreed.

They walked out into the field, to the river's edge where the sunlight glittered like diamonds on the ripples the wind stirred up. The sky brightened to a serene blue. Birds sang from trees and bushes. The morning grew later; Alyssa and William waited.

As the midday hour approached and Alyssa began to fear that Heather had not been healed at all, the sound of hoofbeats interrupted the symphony of wind, river, and birdsong. Her brother Robert rode up to them, his face somber.

"What has happened?" Alyssa asked, rising from her seat on a large river rock. "My baby? Heather?"

"Both well and growing stronger," Robert assured her as he pulled his horse to a stop. "Alyssa, I have sad news. Lord Gavin was at breakfast when he discovered that you and his daughters were gone. His servants say he became enraged. In the midst of his shouts and threats, his face turned purple and he fell to the floor. He is dead, sister."

Alyssa gasped, her hand reaching for her throat as it closed on her. "Dead?" she whispered. "My husband!"

William's face was stony. "He was a cruel man," he said simply.

"He was kind to me, and gentle," Alyssa whispered as tears blurred her sight. "I know what my future was, after Amber's birth, but I loved the man I thought he was, that he pretended to be. Love does not die. It endures, even if the recipient is gone, or never truly existed."

"The price has been paid, young mother," the river whispered. "Go to your children. Raise them to love and not fear, to give and not demand, to know joy despite any sadness. You have the river's blessing."

William took Alyssa's hand and helped her down from her river rock. Robert took her other hand. Together her brother and her son led her back to her waiting daughters.

It is said among the villagers that their village was blessed on the sad day that Lord Gavin died. From that day forward, the frivolous parties that Lord Gavin had thrown were no more. Games were played in the vast gardens of the estate. The orchards and fields were opened for the villagers to use; whatever they grew they could keep. The many empty rooms sheltered the temporarily homeless of the village, and the money that Lord Gavin's estate continued to earn went to helping the village.

When the king's family came for their summer retreat the following year, Ginnia caught the eye of the eldest prince. The king and queen found no objection to his choice, and Ginnia blossomed under his gentle attentions. The following summer a simple wedding was held, and one guest of remarkable beauty caused many whispers, and more than one sideways look when shimmers seemed to trail at her back.

Alyssa did not marry again, but found her life full and happy with her four children and, in time, grandchildren to love, and, it seemed, the whole village to mother. She became known as Stepmother by all in the village save one: her own dear Amber.

Ameria Lewis lived the life of an American gypsy for most of her adult life, floating from state to state as the whim and wish took her. But regardless of her physical address, she's had a permanent home in daydreams and writing. Ameria has run a writing club for nearly 20 years, currently attends college as a non-traditional student, and won NaNoWriMo for the first time in 2013. She is currently pausing in northwest Louisiana, for who knows how long.

To Grandmother's House

Pamela McNamee

"I'm stopping by the mall to pick up a book I ordered before going to help Grandma with her gardening. She'll probably want me to stay for dinner. If I can't catch the last bus, I'll give you a call to come get me. Love you, too." Julie pushed her phone closed, grateful to end the call. After hearing her youngest brother screaming in the background, she was glad to be out of the house for a while, even if it would involve tiring work outside on a hot Saturday in September.

It was shortly past 10:30, so at least she'd have some time to read her book before catching the bus across town. Even if the mall was busy, it would be quieter than home. There weren't many cars in the lot yet, or much traffic, at least not at this corner of the mall away from the food court entrance; that was probably why the bus stopped here.

The central food court area was busy as mall walkers finished their coffee and breakfasts. Julie zigzagged through a brigade of strollers to get to Now and Zen, one of the few independent stores at the mall.

She gagged slightly at the smell of incense as she entered. None was being burned, yet the smell still permeated the air.

"Julie! It's been too long, girl!" came the greeting from Nadine, the 18 year old daughter of the owner; she ran the shop on Saturday mornings.

"Hi," Julie replied, "I can't stay long. I am here to actually buy something this time, though."

Nadine smiled "Yeah, I saw you had Dad order *Wings of an Eagle* for you. Let me know if you like it. We ordered a couple other copies to sell; we like to support local authors."

As usual, Nadine chatted on without much encouragement as she rang up the book. Julie paid and said she'd stop in to talk again soon, then headed back to the food court.

Ricky circled the parking lot looking for a good space. He thought about parking back among the employee spaces since there wouldn't be much traffic there until the afternoon, but he opted for a close space behind the trash dumpster since almost nobody parked near those. He was driving his dad's old Grand

Marquis. Though his dad didn't mind him driving it and adding extra speakers, a CB radio, and other audio stuff, Ricky would never hear the end of it if somebody scuffed it in a parking lot. His dad probably wouldn't even know he'd made the trip since he was away on business this weekend, yet it was still best to be cautious. Hopefully he'd find something quickly and be on his way. Shopping wasn't his favorite thing, yet it was early enough in the day that a run to the mall shouldn't take too long or be stressful. He'd resigned himself to going since some things couldn't be found online, and sometimes you needed things right away; malls could be good for that.

Once inside, Ricky browsed through the game store and the electronics store, yet didn't buy anything. None of the new games appealed to him, and he mostly played online anyway. It was starting to feel like it might be a wasted trip, yet there were still a lot of other things to see.

Heading towards the other end of the mall he passed a group of girls talking at the entrance to a clothing store. They hushed, staring as he walked by, and started giggling. He really hated it when that sort of thing happened. He shoved his hands in his pockets and continued on, looking at the floor.

"They think they're better than me," he thought, "and they don't even know me. Nobody does."

He looked around the food court where lines had started to form for lunch. Why people would go to the mall to eat didn't make sense to him. Why not eat your own food at home and make a shorter trip? He went to use the restroom, watching people going about their lives oblivious to him. Then, when he came out, he saw her.

She was sitting on a bench next to an escalator, casually twisting a stray piece of her pony-tailed hair as she read a book. She looked about five years younger than him, likely still in high school. She was poised, and relaxed, like she didn't have a care in the world.

Ricky averted his gaze and walked around the promenade. He kept glancing at her, seeing her from all sides. He went down the stairs and his heartbeat quickened as he crossed to go up the escalator. He got a good look at her ring free hands when he passed within two feet of her, and he noticed the bus schedule with some times circled that she was holding for a bookmark. She didn't reek of perfume and was dressed simply in scuffed sneakers, jeans, and a t-shirt with a thin flannel shirt. Most people probably ignored her, too. He couldn't though; she was like a dream.

A mix of thoughts ran through his head. He wanted to take a chance—maybe he needed to do so—yet he felt conflicted. He went back to the parking lot, quickly, arguing with himself the whole way.

Julie's phone dinged to remind her she had 20 minutes to catch the bus. She sighed, and closed her book. She wasn't thrilled about gardening, yet knew she'd feel bad if she didn't help, especially after Grandma's heart trouble the previous year. Mom couldn't do much with the other kids in tow, and it did give Julie a bit of a break. She put the book in her bag and decided to walk outside since the weather was nice, and it would be less crowded.

The sun was bright as she stepped outside, and she blinked as her eyes adjusted. She followed the sidewalk towards the bus stop, hoping the A/C on the bus would be working.

"Excuse me miss, could you help me for a minute? I seem to be in a bit of a pickle," a soft spoken young man, with an accent she couldn't place, called from the next row of cars. He looked only a little older than her, and rather cute.

She glanced around, startled. "Uh, I don't think I can; I'm in a bit of a hurry."

He looked a little hurt, and anxious as he came over and stopped about ten feet ahead, directly in her path. He was tall, tanned, and looked rather strong. He blocked the sun as she approached. She squinted against the surrounding glare as she looked up at his face. He smiled at her and wistfully said, "Are you sure?"

She thought to herself that if she were the one needing help she'd be really frustrated to be dismissed out of hand. So she asked, "What's wrong?"

He sighed. "Well, I'm driving my daddy's car and I guess I must've driven over a nail or glass or something cuz I came out and there's a flat tire. I've got everything to change it, yet the lug wrench is stuck in its bracket and these hands of mine just don't fit back there to get a grip on it. It's just over there, and I'd be obliged if you could lend a hand to free it up for me. My daddy's gonna blame me for sure, and he's only gonna be more upset if he has to find somebody to get him down here to fix it."

Julie thought about it. She was sure she still had ten minutes before the bus should arrive, and it was usually late. He seemed sincerely in need, a little scared even, and it sounded simple. Her mom had taught her to change a flat last year, yet this guy looked like he could manage that part himself. "Do unto others," she thought, "and be the change you want to see."

"I'll try it," she said aloud, "yet only for a minute; I don't want to miss my bus."

He smiled at her brightly. "Well thank you, miss, you're like an angel sent straight from heaven."

She was a little taken aback by his compliment. Yet she followed him across the parking rows, fortunately also in the direction of the bus stop.

He headed toward a gray car that had a flat tire on the left rear. A canvas bag and tire were on the ground in a small extra space between the spot the car was in and a brown trash dumpster that hid it from the view of the mall. The trunk was slightly open and he lifted it the rest of the way. "The wrench is pinned at the back, I can nudge it but can't pull it free."

Julie stepped over beside him thinking it would only take a few seconds.

Suddenly, a car slowed to a stop behind them and a girl called out, "Hey Julie, did you finally find yourself a boyfriend?!"

One of the passengers said, "Good one, Jess!"

Everybody in the car laughed as they drove away.

Julie could feel her face turning bright red. She could hardly breathe, yet stammered, "I … I'm sorry about that."

"They friends of yours?" he asked.

She couldn't even look at him. "No, but they know me from school. I'm not their kind of person."

He reached around her, rubbed her shoulder, and said, "Well, I think you're a better kind of person. Don't pay them no mind." He gently put his hand under her chin and lifted it so she had no choice but to meet his eyes. "Any guy'd be lucky to have you as a girlfriend anyhow."

Julie wasn't comfortable being so near him or with him touching her, and she pulled away from him.

He quickly let go and apologized. "I'm sorry! Julie, is it? I didn't mean to scare ya. I'm Ricky."

He stepped back a little, holding out his hand, and she shook it. "Uhm, hi. It's okay; let's just get this over with so you can be on your way."

She leaned over and looked in the trunk. It was dark, yet she could make out the shiny handle of the lug wrench over the shelf area at the back. She reached in and couldn't even touch it.

"I climbed in to get it, yet couldn't get my hand around it," Ricky said, and he held out his hand to help her do the same.

She couldn't turn her head to see it and stretched her arm across the shelf, feeling for it. "Seems like a bad design to put it there."

"I think I've got a screwdriver in my bag; maybe you could pry it off with that," Ricky said, and she heard him unzipping something. She found the end of the wrench and was almost able to grip it.

"Here we are," said Ricky, and she felt his body press against her side as he knelt and reached in around her. "Just hold still while I get this in place."

She felt something soft press against her face that was suddenly in her mouth and being tightened around her head.

Julie pushed back with all her strength, screaming as best she could despite the gag. Yet his body pinned hers against the shelf and forced her completely into the trunk.

"You're an angel," he said, "and I don't want to hurt you none. You and me both, we're real, and I can see you've never had nobody really care about you. You deserve to be noticed, and I'm gonna treat you real sweet."

She let herself fall to the trunk floor, on top of her bag, and pulled up her legs to kick at him. Yet he hooted with laughter. Pushing his knee into her back, he grabbed her feet. She panicked at the sound of tape being pulled off a roll and torn as he bound her ankles together. She flailed with her free arm, screeching in hopes that someone would hear and bring help.

"We're going for a bit of a ride, Julie. You be careful; I don't want nothing bad to happen to you." The knee pressure was gone, yet with one hand he held her down as he stood back on the ground. She pushed up, hoping to scramble back out, yet the trunk lid closed and she was in the dark.

The sound of an air compressor buzzed and Julie felt the left side of the car lift. She was terrified, could hardly breathe, and didn't know what to do. She stopped screaming and pounded the inside of the trunk lid. It was spongy, like some kind of dense foam. She tried to untie the cloth that was gagging her, yet the back of it was wet and unyielding. She realized with horror that he'd planned this whole thing, even deflating his own tire.

She tried kicking the trunk lid, yet that didn't make much noise either. She heard soft thuds on the other side of the trunk wall. The car rocked a little, a door closed, and the car engine roared to life. She heard the exhaust rumbling below her. The car backed up, turned to the right, and stopped. She cried out in frustration as she heard the unmistakable sound of a diesel bus coming to a stop.

Julie pounded on the lid again, yet couldn't notice any effect. Nobody would be able to hear. Then he was driving away. He made a bunch of turns that she couldn't follow.

"I think he's trying to throw off my sense of direction," she thought, "and it's working."

She closed her eyes, willing herself to not cry and to be calm so she could think better. Panic had not helped. She took a deep breath in through her nose, held it, and slowly exhaled from her mouth. The trunk smelled a bit like gym socks, wet grass, mulch, and maybe gasoline or some other solvent. It wasn't pleasant, yet not sickening either.

She took a few more deep breaths, noticing light from where the lock should be. She felt for a latch or other release, yet there wasn't one. She tried kicking at the right where a tail light should be, yet it was tough with her ankles bound together. She lay sideways, pulled her knees to her chest, and started tearing at the duct tape binding them, wishing her fingernails were sharper. The car made a few more turns, and after a brief stop accelerated to what seemed like highway speed.

Ricky was giddy. He couldn't stop smiling as he replayed the events in his mind as he headed home. He loved that this mall had its own highway exit, it reduced some risks and made the trip easier for him.

Sure, he'd taken a little chance by not taping her hands, yet there hadn't been much time. Besides, if he hadn't been able to get out of the locked trunk before it was sure to hold a little gal like her. She wouldn't be able to run off or scream loudly, and he could handle anything else. He liked that she had a bit of fight in her, though, that showed a lot of promise.

It was taking a lot of effort not to panic again in the dark. Not having a set time to be at her grandmother's house meant nobody would miss her for hours. Then, feeling rather dumb, Julie remembered her cell phone.

She pulled it out, and the light from it briefly blinded her. Feeling she'd wasted precious time, she dialed

911 and heard a recording to stay on the line for assistance. When a live operator answered, she tried saying, "Help Me!" yet the gag was too thick and tightly tied to allow more than a hoarse screech.

The operator asked her to repeat what was said, and she tried. He asked her to stay on the line, yet Julie felt like it wasn't working and she should try something else.

She texted her mom, *"Am in the trunk of a gray 4 door car. Some guy grabbed me at the mall while I was on my way to catch the bus. Think we're on a highway. I'm scared. I love you."* Then she sent, *"Tried 911, but there is something tied around my mouth. Help."*

She hoped her mom would think to check her messages soon. She didn't have many other contacts in her phone and most of them didn't text at all. She felt the car slow and go around a curve and shoved the phone in her pocket to hide it, in case they were going to stop.

She tried again to tear at the duct tape, and succeeded in getting off a small amount, yet he'd wrapped it around several times. She'd need to peel it layer by layer or cut it, yet she didn't have a knife of any kind. She had her house keys, and she fumbled through her bag to find them. As she started trying to blindly saw and pierce the tape, she heard her mom's ringtone. She shoved the keys in her other pocket, pulled out the phone, and opened it.

"Is this some kind of a joke, Julie?" her mom started. "I don't think it's funny and I sure don't have time for games!"

Julie gasped and screeched for help, feeling the tears and panic starting to overwhelm her.

"Julie?" Her mom sounded concerned.

Julie murmured, "Yes, help me!" yet doubted her mom could understand her any better than the 911 person.

"Uhm, okay honey, if this isn't a joke, I'm sorry. I love you too. Please say this is a joke. If you can't talk, I hope you'll text me again. I don't know how to help, but if you don't tell me this is a joke right away I'm going to hang up and call 911 myself."

Julie realized she was hyperventilating, and gasped as best she could, "Please, help me."

She heard the phone go silent, and put it away. She tried again to free herself from the duct tape, yet it was hard to get pressure there. Her hands were sweaty, and the keys kept slipping.

"I need to act smarter, not harder," she thought. It was getting hot in the trunk, intensifying the smells and sweat started to run down her face. She wiped it off on her shirt sleeve and tried pulling at the gag again without success.

She had no idea how long she'd been in the trunk. She checked her phone and realized it was only 15 minutes after the bus should have left the mall. She wondered how far they had come. She closed her eyes and concentrated on her breathing.

Julie felt through everything in her bag and pockets and couldn't find anything that might help her. She didn't have any tools. She felt around in the trunk and realized that Ricky had cleared it out pretty well. Duct tape covered over edges of the carpeting and a few broader areas. Maybe she could free that lug wrench after all. She felt along it, thinking there must be a bracket holding it in place by tension. Yet there wasn't. She opened her phone, and its light revealed there was a bracket around the middle of the wrench, screwing it to the back wall of the trunk.

"A totally pre-planned setup," she thought. "Has he done this before, to someone else?"

She used her keys to pry at the bracket itself and popped one of the screws out of the wall. The wrench wouldn't come free, though.

Taking a few more deep breaths, she began to take out the screw by hand from the bracket. The car hit a bump and the wrench rattled loudly. She was thrown forward, hitting her head as the car suddenly slowed and pulled to the right, stopping.

She heard the crackle of a radio speaker mounted above the shelf.

"Now, now, Miss Julie. I don't know what you're doing back there, but my Daddy's gonna be really unhappy if anything happens to his car. It's precious to him, you see. But you're precious to me, like a jewel. You don't mind if I call you Jewel, do you? You're just as pretty as a diamond and your cheeks flush so nice like a ruby in the sunlight when you get embarrassed.

"I know you're scared, yet this really is the best way for you to get home with me. You'll understand when we get there, and it'll be fun. I promise. I'm sure you have a really great smile; I can't wait to see it. You settle down, and you'll be safe and out of there soon, honey."

Julie's heart was in her throat. She didn't know what Ricky intended, and she didn't want to know. She knew she wanted to get out of there and be almost anywhere else.

The car drove on, regaining speed. She held the

wrench still, wrapping it with part of her shirt, as she finished freeing it. Finally, she had it loose.

She figured she might only get one chance to use it, and didn't want to waste it. First she texted her mom again, "*Still in trunk. He's crazy.*" Then she called 911.

She almost cried when a recording said, "Please hold, this number is flagged for immediate police dispatch."

She had no idea what that meant, yet she had no intention of hanging up unless the car stopped.

A new voice said, "Hello, is this Julie Deveroux?"

She tried to say "Yes!"

The voice continued "I'll take that as a yes. You don't have to say more, especially if you think it would be unsafe. Please keep your phone on. Hide it if necessary. Help is on the way, and we can track you by your phone. I'm officer Pete Smithson, by the way. You've been traveling north on Highway 15 towards Elksburg. We don't know which gray car you are in but your mom told us that much.

"Local police will have a roadblock in place in about 10 minutes, yet we don't know if he's taking you that far. There are 3 exits before it, and lots of wooded areas where it would be hard to find folks on foot.

"If you can remember the make and model of the

car or anything else that would distinguish it, that would help. If you think of something and can safely text your mom, she's got my partner's direct number. She called to let us know you'd texted again.

"You're a smart, brave girl. Hang in there Julie; help is getting closer. We'll keep this line open. If he keeps to the highway, you should have a signal."

Julie wasn't sure when she'd started crying again. Her throat hurt, and she couldn't see. She could hardly think. She could hear background noises even though the officer had stopped talking.

She felt around the tail light areas as best she could and used her keys to pry open a seam in the carpet behind the left one. She felt some plastic housing for wires and pulled it loose, hoping it would disable the lights. She shuffled her body around to do the same on the other side. She felt around to identify the brake light itself and braced the end of the lug wrench in the middle of it, positioning it so she could kick at it sideways. She had no reason to think Ricky or his "Daddy" wouldn't hurt her, and doing anything to escape now seemed better than waiting until they got "home."

She kicked as hard as she could. The car shook a little, or so she thought, and red light filtered into the trunk as the wrench broke through and cracked the back of the tail light assembly. She reached down and turned the wrench, whacking it through as best she could to widen the gap. She scrunched down and forced the wrench firmly into the breach. She heard a cracking sound. She braced it again, gave another good kick, and it went through to the outside yet was firmly stuck. She breathed a sigh of relief, relishing the feeling of cooler air from the outside reaching her face. She couldn't see much, yet the light and the air alone made her feel freer and hopeful.

The speaker crackled again. "How you doing back there, Jewel? You still awake? We're almost home, honey. Just another exit to go. I'm so sorry for sticking you back there; I'd much rather be holding you. I'll make it all better soon."

The way he sounded so sincere, concerned, and soothing while doing such a horrible thing made her feel sick and hurt her brain. He was crazy even though he seemed nice. She felt slightly guilty because she had felt special when he complimented her. She didn't want to think about what might happen to him. She didn't want him to suffer. She only wanted to be back with her family.

"Julie, are you listening? This is officer Smithson again. We've got an officer in an unmarked Mustang following a gray sedan that seems to have something sticking out of its right tail light and only the cyclops light works when the brakes are used. We're guessing you're in there, and you're a brave, brave, clever girl.

"Others are on the way from both directions, and things might get more exciting in a few minutes. Hang in there, Julie. We don't know if he's armed or not, but our officers will be. We'll put the car over for the tail lights, and we'll search it. If you're in it, we'll get you out; don't worry. If you can keep quiet so he doesn't panic, that may help."

The car slowed and veered to the right.

"Julie, he's taking an exit. Don't worry, we've got one car right behind him and even if it takes a few extra minutes the rest will be there quickly."

Julie thought her heart might explode from the strain of waiting. The car finished curving and went immediately to the left and slowed to a stop, she could hear the clicking of a turn signal. Then she heard a siren chirp close by and the sound of a door closing.

The speaker behind her crackled. "I'm not sure what this officer wants, Jewel, but you sit tight back there and don't go making no noise. I don't want to have to hurt anybody, but I'm not going to let them take my angel away from me."

The car turned off. Julie shuddered and waited. The gag was making her jaw hurt, and she really needed a drink of water. She strained to hear, yet the conversation was muffled. The heat was getting to her head, and she felt a little sleepy, yet she jolted awake when she heard a commanding voice sharply say, "Please step out of the car sir!"

The car shifted and squeaked as Ricky got out, then all was quiet. She heard scuffling, and a voice crying out in pain. The car rocked as something heavy fell onto it, twice. Then she heard, "Drop the knife, boy. It's over. Drop it, or I shoot!"

She heard more sirens, and the screeching of tires. Then, the sweetest sound she'd heard all day, the trunk release clicked and the lid popped open. She pushed it as high as it would go, sitting up. Police cars lined the opposite side of the road, and one was directly behind the car she was in. She looked around and saw the Mustang had pulled in directly in front of it at an angle. She saw Ricky kneeling on the ground near the road, with his hands cuffed behind him and two policemen talking to him. He turned his head, revealing red puffiness swelling his face from his cheekbones to his chin. Another officer was putting a long thin knife into a bag. A paramedic was helping an officer remove a blood-soaked shirt.

"Take it slow and easy, Julie," said a woman in uniform standing next to the car, "It's over. You're safe. He can't hurt you now. Let me cut you loose from this and we'll have a medical person check you. Okay?"

Julie nodded, and was freed.

The next several weeks were a blur of meetings with police officers, doctors, counselors, and lawyers.

Each one had Julie reliving at least part of the most unpleasant experience of her life. She moved in with her grandmother for about a year and a half to avoid the public attention that stemmed from her story hitting social media and becoming national news. Some people considered her a hero and many offered support of one form or another. Yet there were also frightening messages saying it was a shame she'd escaped. It was all too much at the time. Eventually her family moved to a different state with a new last name for a fresh start.

It took months before a court ordered that Richard

Jarvis, Jr. be confined to a secure mental health facility. It was almost a year before federal agents had Richard Jarvis, Sr. in custody for a range of allegations including kidnapping, rape, and murder.

Julie had nightmares from time to time for decades. She considered each one a way for her mind and spirit to work through all the what-ifs without them taking over her conscious thoughts. She was grateful for her escape and determined not to let even her own mind keep her a prisoner.

Pamela McNamee worked as a computer systems specialist at Boston area colleges specializing in distance learning. She transitioned to working as a home-based independent contractor when her first child was born. She enjoys camping, gaming, and learning to cook ethnic foods.

Cinder-Stepmother

Susan Bianculli

I opened my eyes to near pitch darkness. That was not unusual in and of itself, though. The faded velvet curtains of my four poster bed were always drawn tightly closed to ward off the morning chill of the manor house, since any fire laid in the fireplace grate at night was always out come morning no matter how well I'd banked it. But it was sunrise; my internal clock told me that.

Under the large patch-quilted coverlet that had kept me warm as I slept, I rolled onto my back and stretched out my arms and legs to banish the sleep cramps and bring some energy back into them. My fingers brushed the yellow linen covered pillows beside mine, and my eyes filled with slow tears as they had on many previous mornings. My darling Stepfen, the older country gentleman who had swept me off my feet just three years ago, would never sleep beside me again.

Our marriage of two and a half years had been

wonderful, marred only by Stepfen's three children from his previous wife. Well, actually, marred only by one of them. His two youngest children, Drussella and Anastaizella, had taken to me right away and made me feel like one of the family. They had even gone so far as to call me 'mama', and I loved them for that and for many other things. His eldest, Cindiella, was far less welcoming. She'd never forgiven me for being only five years older than herself, for replacing her mother in her father's bed, for being treated like a grownup lady when she wasn't, and many other such things beyond my control.

But with Sir Stepfen dead these past six months, I was left a very young widow with three stepchildren of whom I was determined to take good care.

Crash!

I sat bolt upright, heart pounding. My oaken bed-room door had been slammed open with a resounding thud. But as nothing else happened after that, I knew what sight would greet me when I opened the curtain. I wiped my eyes free of tears and then poked my head out, pretending unconcern.

Cindiella stood on the door's threshold with a men-dacious grin. "Good morning, Stepmother Trelainne.

Sleep well?" she asked with a false sweetness.

She was already dressed for work in a grey shirt, a short brown over-frock, and a grey apron dirtied from the day before.

"Why, of course," I replied pleasantly. "How could I not, seeing that I am so well loved that my beloved step-daughter comes to start my fire for me every morning?"

She lost her grin at that. If she were to come to my bedroom early every morning, she would have to clean and light my fireplace. She didn't have to come, but she liked scaring me awake more than she hated tending the fire. She had reveled that first week after Stepfen's death in my shrieks of fear each morning, which had led to our current arrangement. I had supposed it was some sort of way of getting her grief out, which is why I didn't put a stop to it. That's why I tried to wake up before the inevitable every sunrise now.

Cindiella, mad that I hadn't screamed today, stomped over to the fireplace and started cleaning out the ashes. I slid out my red velvet wrap from under my coverlet where it had retained my body's warmth, and pulled it around me before getting out of bed to retrieve my work clothes from my armoire. Lady or no, an estate didn't look after itself. We all worked hard to keep it prosperous, even though Cindiella often had other views of what was proper for her to do as her part.

In Cindiella's defense, though, Stepfen's first wife and the girls' biological mother had been the spoiled daughter of a Count from the court. Stepfen had left her alone for much of the children's younger years while fighting in the wars of the kingdom. The girls' mother had taught her children that they didn't need to do anything for themselves; that they would be provided for because they were nobility. That all changed when she had broken her neck from a fall down the main steps of the manor house and Stepfen had come home to take care of his family and his estate. He had been horrified when told flat out by a then eight-year-old Cindiella that she was too good to do work. Stepfen immediately had dismissed the extra servants that had somehow accumulated in his absence and instituted a radical change in how the household ran.

Under his direct supervision the estate had grown even more prosperous. Over the following years the girls had grown more used to the new regime, especially the younger ones, but it was a fact that Cindiella, now at fifteen years of age, still needed a firm hand directing her to do the work she was assigned. Stepfen had married me not only because he liked my looks and my personality when we'd met at a May Day celebration, but also because I was a farmer's daughter and well used to doing chores.

Loud banging noises came from behind me in the direction of my fireplace. I winced at them as I quickly slid into my dress and did up the buttons on the front. At least it seemed I didn't have to nag Cindiella about finishing the job this morning.

"Done!" she snarled behind me as I heard her hurl the fireplace poker back into its holder.

I turned around and forced a smile to my face to thank her but gasped instead. "Cindiella! What on earth …?"

She was all over ashes, like she'd dumped the contents of the fireplace on herself.

"The stupid scuttle tipped and spilled all over me, and I dropped it," she whined, and kicked the empty brass ash bucket on the hearth accusingly. "But what do you care? You never even so much as turned around to look!"

My face and neck flushed red with guilt. She was right.

"I'm sorry," I started to say, but she interrupted me.

"Don't offer me your false apologies!" she said, angry tears leaving trails in the smut on her face as she stomped her foot. "You don't care for me! You don't care about anything except how to figure out how to make my life even more miserable! I could have had my foot broken when the scuttle fell on it, but you would never have even noticed! You would have probably left it to heal deformed! You are a horrible old witch that somehow enchanted my father to turn against me and then to die and leave me, and I hope you will pay for it someday!"

She turned and ran out the opened door, leaving me speechless. In the hallway I heard giggling from Drussella and Anastaizella, who must have opened their bedroom doors at all the racket. I heard them tell their sister she looked more like a Cinder-ella than a Cindi-ella. As I took a step towards my door, incoherent screaming sounded from the hallway. I rushed out to protect the girls from each other and heard a slam before I even crossed the threshold. I found poor Anastaizella sitting on her rump in her doorway, bawling, with Drussella crouching beside her, arms around her sister's shoulders. Cindiella's door was firmly shut.

I sighed and went to the younger girls.

"Mama! Mama! Cindiella pushed me down!" Anastaizella cried through her tears.

"She did! She did!" confirmed Drussella.

I picked up Anastaizella and hugged her. "I know, darling. Cindiella is going through a rough patch at the moment, that's all. We just need to give her time."

"She's always going through a rough patch," observed Drussella with a sour face.

"Go get dressed, girls, and I'll meet you in the kitchen for breakfast," I said with as straight a face as I could manage at Drussella's observation as I put her sister down.

The two girls scurried away when I went to my eldest step-daughter's door and knocked on it.

"Cindiella!"

No reply.

I tried again. "Cindiella? How could you do that? Drussella is younger than you by a good bit. You need to open the door now and apologize for pushing your sister, young lady."

Silence was still my answer.

I waited several minutes before raising my voice and saying, "Fine! Then as punishment for your behavior and attitude, you are to sweep and wash the grand hall and then take down the curtains and beat them free of dust, all by yourself, in addition to doing your regular chores."

I heard a crash inside the room against the door and guessed Cindiella must have thrown her pewter vase at it again. The poor vase was quite dented from its regular abusive treatment at the hands of its owner, but I was unwilling to replace it until my stepdaughter outgrew this particular phase.

"That's so unfair!" she screamed from within.

"Had you ignored your sisters' words, this wouldn't have happened. The punishment stands," I replied with firmness. "Come down and eat when you feel you can be more civil."

I swept down the stairs to assist Cook in getting breakfast on the table for everybody, leaving Cindiella to shriek in anger in her room behind me.

Things went downhill from there. Cindiella needed much more oversight than usual in doing her chores, which severely cut into my own. My throat grew dry constantly reminding her how to best sweep and mop the grand hall, and by the time she'd gotten around to taking down the curtains I was gritting my teeth. At least I could do some of my own work, such as mending clothes and teaching the younger girls how to darn socks, while supervising Cindiella out in the garden with the drapes.

To my surprise, sometime later a hunting horn sounded out in front of the manor house. Reminding Cindiella to continue what she was doing and cautioning Drussella and Anastaizella to not prick themselves while I was gone, I ran around front. A royal messenger on his big bay horse sat there waiting to be met by someone from the estate. He threw an envelope at me like it was a discus as soon as I rounded the corner. He took off before it was halfway to me, the horse's iron shod hooves spraying the dirt and sand of the drive in his hurry; a leather bag full of similar envelopes slung across his shoulders banging at his side. I caught the heavy, gilt edged missive before it hit the ground and opened it right away, guessing it was important. I scanned it, gasped, and ran back to the garden.

"Girls! Girls! There's to be a royal ball tonight in honor of Prince Albert's coming-of-age!" I said with excitement as I got back to them.

The two younger girls jumped up and clapped their hands enthusiastically, and Cindiella, a smile on her face for the first time in quite a while, dropped her rug beater to the ground.

I frowned at her. "You're not done with the curtains yet, young lady. Pick that up. Before I will even consider allowing you to go, you need to be done with everything."

The smile fled from her lips. "What?"

Drusella and Anastaizella hid behind my work skirts at the mutinous expression on their sister's face.

"You heard me," I replied, staring her down.

She deliberately ignored both the beater and my words, turned around, and marched with a stiff back towards the house.

"Cindiella! If you walk away now, you will not be allowed to go to the ball even if you do finish all your chores!" I warned.

She ignored me and slammed the kitchen door behind her as she entered the house.

I felt a tug on my skirts. "Mama? Will you really not let Cindiella go to the ball?" Drussella asked.

I sighed. "Yes, my dear. Cindiella needs to learn that work comes before play, and that I mean what I say. If she'd come back, all would have been well. But she's, well ..."

"Stubborn!" piped up Anastaizella.

I smiled and ruffled her hair. "Yes. She is. Sadly.

Now, to work, girls, or you won't be able to go to the children's party, or I to the main ball. The same holds true for us, you know."

"Yes, Mama!" they chorused.

Evening came, and the younger girls' and my chores were done early enough that we'd had time to bathe and dress in our good clothes. My fancy dark grey dress and light grey head scarf were somewhat out of date, but they were still presentable enough for an occasion like this. Drussella had chosen to wear a dress of greens and Anastaizella in one of purples, and I would not have been able to pick which one was the cuter. They joined me in the front hall in front of the opened double doors to wait for the coachman to come around.

"Wait for me!" came a familiar voice from up the stairs, sounding happy and excited.

We turned and looked. Cindiella swept down the stairs wearing a hideous gown. It was quite obvious she had made it herself without any help, or even a pattern. The seams were crooked, the colors clashed, the fabric bunched, and the trim that she'd obviously added as an afterthought was already coming undone. She couldn't have done a worse job if she had tried. But it didn't matter, because she had no business being here. I already knew she hadn't finished any of her regular daily chores. I had personally checked earlier.

"Where do you think you are going?" I inquired.

"To the ball, of course, and I'm going to snag myself the royal prince!" she replied gaily as she twirled on the step above the ground floor.

A flounce on her hem parted ways with her dress.

"No, you are not," I said flatly.

Her face fell, and the customary scowl took its place.

"I told you this morning that you needed to do your chores before you could go to the ball. And when you walked away from me in the garden, I told you to come back or I would not allow you to go even if you did them."

Cindiella tried to interrupt but I spoke over her, raising my voice. "Not only did you not come back, you did not do any of your chores. I and your father have told you more than once, young lady, that work comes before play. As you have not worked today, you may not play tonight."

"But that's not fair!" she cried.

She threw a temper tantrum then, which I simply watched. Drussella's and Anastaizella's hands crept into mine as, wide eyed, they watched their sister stomp her feet, shake her fists, and scream herself hoarse. Realizing I would not be swayed, Cindiella finally ran out of the front hall towards the garden, sobbing about how she was always so unfairly put upon. The carriage came up to the stone steps just then, and I ushered the younger girls out to it. We left for the royal ball in blessed silence.

The carriage drive up to the palace was lit by what looked like hundreds of lanterns, making the girls oooh and aaah and bounce with excited anticipation. Upon our arrival at the marble steps that led up to the ornate palace entrance, I was handed out and escorted with the two girls by a footman to the children's section set in the East wing. We were delighted to see that it had been decorated like a country fair, with many booths of free games and food decked out in flower garlands. I was assured by the head server on duty that all the children coming would be heavily supervised, and that I could go and have a good time without a care. The girls squealed with glee and rushed off to join the fun already underway as I thanked the woman in charge. I was then escorted by my footman through the white stone corridors illuminated by white stone sconces to the main ballroom, where he bowed and left me.

It was gorgeous. The many large crystal chandeliers that hung low from the ceiling had been polished to a shine, their facets reflecting the multitude of their candle flames many times over. Large painted floor vases filled with fresh flowers perfumed the air. Red and blue draperies enhanced the pale pink and white of the enormous marble-tiled room. The men's clothes were elegant, and the ladies' dresses dazzling. I was in awe. I walked dreamily down the broad steps and lost myself in the sea of glittering humanity.

After most of the guests had arrived, Prince Albert himself entered the room dressed in a militarily inspired outfit made from white silk and satin and trimmed in red. All the ladies, myself included, stopped what we were doing, made our curtseys, and congratulated him. He was quite handsome, and many a married woman sighed because she could not be considered eligible.

Later, after accepting a crystal glass of punch from yet another server, I could see a stir being made across the ballroom floor. A crowd of people had gathered in a circle, so being naturally curious I went to see what was happening. In the center of it, a beautiful girl whom I hadn't seen before danced with Prince Albert.

I thought she looked familiar, but the Prince and she twirled and circled constantly and prevented me from getting a good look at her face. I could easily see that the mysterious girl wore a silver ball gown that quite outshone everyone else's, with silver elbow length gloves and a hair ribbon to match. I sighed in envy at her ensemble, wishing I had one like it. The Prince danced her out onto the balcony in time to the music of the orchestra, and footmen materialized to guard the Prince's exit. I felt a small pang as I realized from this that the Prince would not put in an appearance again—it would have been nice to dance with him at least once. Determined to make the best of it, I went back to enjoying myself at the ball.

About an hour after midnight, my feet about danced off from my many partners, my yawns made me decide to collect my girls from the children's party and return home. All the children had been bedded down on thick woolen blankets on the floor hours earlier, so two footmen obligingly carried the sleepy Drussella and Anastaizella to my carriage for me.

The next morning I woke up long past dawn. And not to my bedroom door being slammed open like it had been for the last six months, either. It was, instead, to another hunting horn being sounded outside the manor's front door. I grabbed my wrap from under my bed covers and flung it about me as I rushed my feet into velvet slippers and hurried down the main stairs.

The housemaid was just opening the door, and I recognized the Arch Duke Francis outside on the broad top step. He was bearing what looked like a slipper made of glass on a red velvet pillow. I looked at it, confused, as I went to greet him. What on earth was he doing at my front door with something so unwearable? I motioned to the housemaid that I would take it from here, and she silently withdrew.

The horn sounded again, and a herald dressed in red and white royal livery came into view unrolling an official looking scroll.

"Hear ye, Hear ye! It is so demanded by his Royal Majesty, through the person of the Arch Duke Francis, that all women who attended the ball last night must try on this slipper that was left behind to see if it fits! If it does fit, the wearer is then pleaded, through the Arch Duke, to accept Prince Albert's hand in marriage!" he loudly intoned before stepping back out of sight.

The Arch Duke made a suitable bow.

I felt faint. A brief fantasy swept through my head of

living in the palace married to the Prince and being happy, the three girls living with us and treated like royalty.

I came to my senses and addressed the Arch Duke. "I'm sorry, Your Grace, but there is no one here who could have worn that. I and my two younger daughters did go to the ball, but I can assure you that that is not my slipper. And since I know my daughters' clothes, I can also assure you that it is neither of theirs, either."

"My orders, Madam, are to try it on every one who went," he said with polite inflexibility, stroking his bushy black mustache.

I shrugged and moved to let him come in.

"Oh, very well, but you will soon see I am right." I called up the stairs. "Drussella! Anastaizella! Come here, please!"

The two girls came scampering down the stairs in their dressing gowns. I thought I saw Cindiella lurking at the top in the shadows, but I had my hands full with Drussella and Anastaizella barreling into me for hugs to concern myself over her lurking.

Duke Francis, seeing how young they were, realized that what I had said to be true. But he still went through the motions of having all three of us sit down on a foyer chair and trying the slipper on. As expected, it didn't properly fit any of our feet.

"Wait!" cried a voice up the stairs. "May I try it on?"

I frowned, and then turned to the Arch Duke. "That is my other stepdaughter, Your Grace, but she did not go to the ball last night. She has no need to try the slipper on."

"Oh, but you're wrong, stepmother dear!" Cindiella said gaily, almost dancing down the stairs into the front hall.

I stared. She must have been up for hours. Her hair was done up in an elegant swirl, she had applied make-up, her pretty violet dress was clean and fresh, and she smelled faintly of perfumed soap as she sashayed past me and sat down in the chair Anastaizella had just vacated. I was speechless.

Cindiella kicked off a house slipper and held out her admittedly dainty foot to the Arch Duke. He tried it on her—and to everyone's surprise but hers, it fit!

Cindiella turned triumphantly on me. "See! I told you I would go to the ball! And I did, even after you told me I couldn't—my fairy godmother came to me, and gave me a dress and a carriage and everything!"

I narrowed my eyes. A fairy godmother? A mischievous trickster, more like, who'd probably come with cheap tricks and catches after I'd left the premises. But it was too late to warn Cindiella about taking magic from strangers; the damage had been done.

She stood up, and then withdrew from a hidden pocket in her dress a matching glass slipper and put it on as well. A swirl of silvery wisps rose up out of nowhere and engulfed her, and suddenly she was dressed in the beautiful gown, gloves, and hair ribbon I'd admired last night. She preened before us.

"Magic!" whispered the Arch Duke in horror. "You have bewitched the Prince!"

Cindiella laughed while smoothing out her full skirts. "No, I haven't—other than with my looks and my boobs, that is. It's amazing what a guy will give you if you promise him that you will let him touch …." Her eyes drifted to her sisters, and amazingly she didn't finish what I suspected would have been a crude statement.

"Anyhow, Your Grace," she continued, "I believe you have something to ask me?"

The Arch Duke looked reluctant, but he got down on one knee.

"Will you marry Prince Albert, my lady?" he asked her. It looked like it hurt him to say it.

Cindiella threw her arms up in the air and did a happy twirl, skirts flying. "Yes, yes, a thousand times yes!"

He looked at me, and I gave a tiny half-shrug. If she had the chance to marry Prince Albert, I would not stand in her way.

"Then let us go," he said to her. "Please head out to the carriage, my lady. I will join you in a minute."

Cindiella ran out to the carriage without so much as a backwards look at her two sisters or me.

"Madame Trelainne?" he said, taking my hand and bowing over it.

I finally found my voice. "I ... have no words. She didn't come with us to the ball last night, I swear to you. I don't know how this happened. I am so sorry."

He sighed. "What's done is done. The shoe fits, so she must wear it. His Majesty will, of course, settle a generous bridal price on your household. May it allow you to fill her place with someone who can help you in her stead."

Then his eyes twinkled as he looked me up and down. "Of course, I would be honored to bring it myself and assist you in any way I could."

A smile crept to my lips as I assessed him in return. He seemed fit and healthy, was well dressed, and was certainly much younger than my dear, departed Stepfen.

"I would like that, Your Grace. I do promise I will be more suitably attired next time."

He laughed, kissed my hand, and then went out to the carriage that held an impatient Cindiella.

We went out to the front steps and called out good wishes to her as the royal carriage rolled off down the drive.

I ushered Drussella and Anastaizella back inside after the noble party was out of sight, and smiled to myself as I directed the girls down to breakfast. I had slept past dawn for the first time in months, Cindiella was to be suitably married off, we were to get a gift of money for the estate because of her, and the Arch Duke Francis had indicated an interest in me.

Not a bad beginning for a morning at all.

Susan Bianculli. a happily married mother of two living in Georgia, has loved to read all her life. A graduate of Emerson College with a Minor in Writing, she hopes through her stories to share and inspire in young readers the same love of reading that she had at their age, and still has now. You can learn more about her work at susanbianculli.wix.com/home.

Who's Afraid?

Judy Rubin

"Who's afraid?" Chuck called.

"Not me," Willie laughed.

"Or me," Ron grinned.

"Then it's you, Wolf," Chuck yelled.

Wolf knew better than to argue. He couldn't win, not three-to-one. But he could run. And he did.

Over the fence, through Perkin's garden, and into the graveyard was the safest route. He'd done it before.

Slim enough to push through the gate, Wolf slid under the chain, tearing his sleeve, before he sprinted to the crypt. Wolf cowered, but not from fear. He was safe; and, if his plan worked, he'd get revenge.

"So who's afraid?" whispered the wind.

"Not me," howled Wolf.

"Home early," whispered the wind.

"Too early for my liking," croaked the oak, branches swaying wild, tossing leaves like rain.

But Wolf ignored their banter. Nothing was new in their words. Nothing worth hearing as he pried open the crypt. Cool darkness was safe. With only tombs as company, no arguments would haunt his dreams.

"No one sleeps tonight," whispered the wind.

"Then I'll sleep well." Wolf shrugged. "For others think I am no one."

"A diversion," croaked the oak, limbs dipping so low that they brushed against Wolf's cheek. "You're little more than a diversion in the scheme of things."

One limb snapped like thunder, while the wind whispered, "They're near."

Wolf braced. They followed, but they shouldn't have been able to get in. Without a key, the gate protected, kept out intruders. Wolf waited in the shadows, close enough to hear their shrieks.

"Hide," whispered the wind, as Wolf pushed into the crypt and slid between two coffins.

"We know you're in there, Wolf," called Chuck, scraping the door with jagged nails.

"Or is it Chicken?" laughed Ron, as his fist banged against the open door.

As Ron slipped inside, his shadow stretched across the crypt. Wolf choked back excitement as the shadow touched his arm. Cold. Too cold.

"Ghost step on your tomb," Willie laughed, slamming

the door behind him.

"Too late," whispered the wind, sending an icy breeze under the door.

Willie pushed, but the door held tight. Wolf knew it would. He set the trap.

"Who's got a flashlight?" called Chuck. "I told you idiots to bring a flashlight."

"I got a match," Ron said, choking a little with fear, as the wind screamed outside.

Wind and darkness gave an eerie life to the tomb, one known to Wolf, who welcomed its safety, as he slipped deeper within the shadows.

Wolf hid in the crypt to control his rage. He was an easy target to push down stairs and into lockers at school. But not here, not today.

Willie reached out, shrieked, as his hand slipped through a cobweb.

"Get it off! Get it off!" Willie screamed, too late, as a spider crawled into his sleeve, and with a single bite silenced Willie.

"Where are you, Willie?" Chuck called. "Where's that match, Ron?"

With a snap, light flickered, then sizzled in the cool damp of the crypt.

"Light another one," Chuck called, his rage warming with his fear.

"Nooooo!" screamed Ron as he fell across Willie, match singeing the other boy's shirt.

Burnt cloth and flesh merged as Ron swatted the rising smoke. Willie yawned, choked, then lay silent.

"What now?" called Chuck. "You guys are a couple of wimps. You make Wolf look brave."

Wolf slid deeper into the shadows.

"I think Willie's dead," Ron groaned. "He's not moving."

"He fainted, fool," Chuck snorted, stepping over Willie.

Wolf edged toward the door, unseen, until Chuck scraped a match across the stone.

"He's there," Chuck screamed, pushing Ron ahead. "Get him!"

And in that moment, Wolf pressed the hinge and sprinted out the door, pulling it closed after him. He set the bolt in a single snap.

"Who's afraid now?" called Wolf, teeth bared.

But sealed within the crypt, no sound entered, nor was heard, save the wind and scraping branches.

Wolf leaped high, feet planted precariously on the

arch as he laughed, "Three."

"Not enough," whispered the wind.

"Never enough," croaked the oak. "You owe us a debt for your safety."

"But the night is young," Wolf howled, and in two leaps, he was over the fence, on the prowl.

Takes just a limp to look helpless, and that last leap had Wolf favoring his left leg.

But where should he start? Ron, Willie, and Chuck had chased him from school, just like they did every day. But school was out, even after-school sports.

Maybe the mall. Kids usually hung out there, especially the popular ones. Wolf would be easy prey, as would anyone who followed.

Wolf loped along the street, reaching the entrance just as Maggie and Francie shoved past him and giggled through the doors.

"Give me a hand?" Wolf asked, limping behind.

"Looks more like you need a foot," giggled Chelsea, as she pushed past Wolf, knocking him off balance.

Wolf braced, excited with the hunt, then followed them through two candy stores, to the food court, staying just far enough behind to escape their notice. Not that they would have looked for him, or at him. At school, he was little more than a pawn, an easy target. But tonight the game was his, played by his rules.

Phone out, Maggie dialed, but snapped, "No answer," after the third try, adding, "Chuck knows better than to keep me waiting."

"Maybe he's seeing someone else," Chelsea laughed. "I saw him eyeing that new girl in English."

Maggie's sneer stopped Chelsea.

But Francie picked up with, "The blue-eyed blond? Willie's been talking about her all week."

Wolf settled two tables away, lifting his sore leg to a chair. But no one noticed. No one ever noticed. If they only knew what he'd done, what he could do. But that didn't matter. He could wait. He knew how to wait.

Wolf coughed back a howl, then said, "I saw Chuck just a while ago. He was with Ron, Willie, and someone else."

"Who?" Maggie sneered, charging to his table, kicking the chair from under his foot.

Wolf shrugged, rubbing his leg, yellow eyes closed to hide his glee, as he said, "I don't know. But I can show you where they are."

Too easy, Wolf thought. But jealousy was all he needed to set his game in motion.

"Forget Chuck," Chelsea mumbled through a mouthful of fudge. "He's a loser."

"You forget him," Maggie shot back. "He's not your boyfriend."

Wolf stood, stretching his left leg, before taking a tentative step.

"Where you going?" snapped Maggie.

"Home," said Wolf, his back to the girls, a smile so wide that he dug his nails into his palms to hold in the joy.

Out the door, Wolf did not look back. He didn't have to. They were easy prey.

Maggie's, "Wait! I told you to wait, stupid," told Wolf that she was near, with Chelsea and Francie close behind. They were never far apart.

"Too easy," whispered the wind.

"Not as easy as you think," whispered Wolf, rounding a corner, gaining speed despite his limp.

"Oak will know," the wind whispered. "He won't be pleased."

"He never is," Wolf mumbled.

"What are you talking about, stupid?" Maggie sneered, closing in on him.

"Just talking to myself," Wolf called back, yellow eyes alight.

"'Cause no one would talk to you, loser," Chelsea laughed, tossing another piece of fudge in her mouth.

Wolf caught his breath, bit back a curse.

"Not so fast," Maggie called, struggling after him.

But Wolf only limped faster, reaching the cemetery in minutes.

"He's going through the cemetery," said Chelsea. "No way I'm going in there."

"I told them you wouldn't come in," Wolf said, pushing the gate wide enough to slip through, then pulling it closed behind him.

"You saying we're scared?" Maggie challenged, still not moving toward the gate. No need to get too close. She'd heard tales about blood-sucking bats and knew the boys might be waiting just inside to scare her.

"No," Wolf said, eyes wide. "Chuck said it. Willie and Ron agreed. But only Chuck said it."

"He's a fine one to talk," Maggie said, still not moving. "Can't sleep in the dark. Needs a light, even at the movies."

Wolf shrugged before he limped into the shadows.

"You just leaving us out here?" Maggie yelled.

"Of course, not," Wolf called back. "I'm going to tell the guys you're here. Have them come out."

"And leave us here alone," Chelsea called. "It's dark and cold. You can't just leave us!"

"It's the only way I can get them to come out," Wolf called.

"Not working," whispered the wind. "They're not coming in."

"He doesn't know how to make it work," croaked the oak, tossing leaves at Wolf's face.

"You think you're big," Maggie sneered at Wolf. "You think you're bad. You think you're the big, bad ...."

"Wolf," Chelsea cackled, tumbling against the fence. "You think you're the big bad ...."

"Wolf," said Wolf, yellow eyes barely open. "My name is Wolf."

"But you're so big, so brave," Maggie mocked, staring into the darkness.

But Wolf didn't answer, as he disappeared into the evening mist.

"Don't walk away from me," Maggie shouted, pushing through the gate with Francie close behind. "No one turns his back on me! No one, especially a nobody like you!"

"Trapped," whispered the wind.

"You got her," croaked the oak. "And the others will

follow. Maybe there is hope for you."

"Don't leave me out here," Chelsea whined, pushing through the gate after Francie.

"Not so easy for that one," whispered the wind.

"Almost plump enough to fill a tree," croaked the oak.

But Wolf never turned as he trotted toward the crypt with the three girls, breathless, stumbling behind.

Wolf's keen ears heard Chuck scratching at the door, with Ron screaming, "Let us out! Let us out, or else! Wolf, let us out or you'll pay!"

"Or else what," Wolf mumbled, leaping atop the crypt.

"You hear me?" Maggie called again. "No one walks away from me, loser."

Maggie rounded the crypt to find Wolf perched on the arch.

"You look like a fool," Chelsea giggled, barely able to catch her breath.

Wolf measured the width of the crypt with his stride, while trapped below, Chuck moaned, "Okay. You win. Just let us out."

"He lies," whispered the wind.

"Best to leave them," croaked the oak. "They'll make fine mulch."

Wolf bit back a chuckle, while Maggie paced below.

Fists hit the door, but Maggie heard no voices from within. Chelsea strained to hear, while Francie backed away, and the wind blew wild.

A single branch snapped, dropping against the door, while above Wolf crouched. A leap had him at Maggie's feet.

"What's wrong with you?" Maggie shrieked, shoving Wolf. "You think you're so bad. You're nothing. Do you hear me? You're nothing."

"I thought you wanted to see Chuck," Wolf smirked. "Thought you wanted to see who he's with, who that other person is."

"Fool," Maggie hissed, pushing against the door. No movement, just squeals from within and a dull scratch against wood.

'Have it your way,' Wolf shrugged. "I have things to do."

"Huff and puff," Chelsea laughed, pushing past Maggie, adding her weight to the door.

A final push had the door open.

"'Bout time," Chuck snarled, running past Chelsea, Ron and Willie right behind.

"Don't go," Wolf snarled. "We're not through here.

I thought you said you were brave."

"Idiot," Chuck snapped, fist set to connect with Wolf's jaw, 'til a wind gust caught the oak's branch and set it careening between Wolf and Chuck. Wild winds slapped branches against Chuck's face, ripped at his arm. Ron and Willie faired no better, with brittle leaves cutting into their faces.

"Wind," yelled Wolf. "Watch out. Another branch."

Crackling branches sent boys and girls into the crypt. A single gust blew shut the door.

Wind and oak promised a safe home. All they asked was a sacrifice or two, and Wolf readily complied.

"Done," whispered the wind.

"Never believed you could do it," croaked the oak.

"But I did," smiled Wolf. "I'm the big bad wolf. Don't expect anything less. And if you do, then why don't you huff and puff and blow the crypt down. I've got more than three little pigs. I've got six squealing kids, and with any luck, tomorrow I'll have more."

"Many more," whispered the wind.

"A dozen will nurture my roots," croaked the oak.

"I'll let them out sooner or later," Wolf said. "After they learn their lesson."

"Later," whispered the wind.

"Much later," croaked the oak.

"Six fewer bullies, and six more tomorrow will stop the terror." Wolf sighed, drawing his nails across the door.

"So you think," whispered the wind.

"Perhaps he's right," croaked the oak. "He's done more than expected."

"I'm big. I'm bad," howled Wolf, arms wide. "I'm the big bad wolf!"

Though **Judy Rubin** lives in Downey, California, she has traveled extensively in Europe, the Middle East, and Asia to research and to gain insight for her manuscripts. With a Master of Arts in literature, as well as standard secondary, community college, and library service credentials, she has worked as a language arts teacher, a storyteller, and a library media teacher from middle school to college levels, as well as provided district level teacher training in storytelling workshops and creative writing techniques.

In Her Arms
Jeanne Kramer-Smyth

I was rattled awake from a dream of sunshine and wildflowers by the vibrations of a large truck driving past my window. The glass shook and my bed shimmied across the floor. I sat up and pulled back the blackout curtains. The bleak landscape of Antarctica jarred my sleep clouded mind. We don't have trucks, only a couple of small snowmobiles in the dome with us.

The sky was light, but it never gets completely dark here during the summer. I let go of the curtain and fumbled for my clock. 3:45 AM.

I switched on my light and tried to wake up. I had fallen asleep with my blanket covered in schoolbooks again. The books began to tilt and slide, thumping to the floor. Scrambling out of bed, I lurched toward the door, almost ending up in the closet. An alarm shrieked to life in the hallway.

Not a truck, an earthquake. What were you supposed to do in an earthquake? Go outside? Get under the desk? The alarm bounced around inside my skull.

I grabbed the doorframe and leaned out into the dim hallway looking toward the room where my father and stepmother slept.

Their doorway was open, and my father pulled himself through it. His gray hair was a wild halo glowing in the light from behind him.

"Lea? Stay there," he called over the alarm's blare. "The doorway is the safest place."

A violent tremor pitched me forward into the hallway. I fell onto my knees on the cool tile. It took me a moment to realize that the sound I was hearing was my own screams. Chunks of the ceiling started to rain down. I curled up on the floor. The air tasted of dust and plaster. I tried not to choke on it and keep breathing. My heart was racing and I wanted to run to my dad, but larger pieces of ceiling were falling now.

I covered my head with my arms. Concrete and light fixtures crashed all around me. Dust showered down, turning my dark skin gray. The blare of the alarm washed over me.

Finally the world stopped shaking. The alarm wailed forlornly for a few more moments, and then it fell quiet too.

I peeked out from beneath my hair. I could see part

of the dim hallway through an opening in the debris near my face. It was criss-crossed with beams and massive blocks of what had been the ceiling and the roof beyond. The low angled sun of early morning lit the slowly settling dust.

That's when I heard Arla-Mia calling me. A machine my father had designed and implanted in her neck let her speak human words. It made her voice rough, like that of an old lady after a life of smoking. I had learned a few of her native words, but I couldn't remember a single one right now.

"Help me!" I called back, before coughing. I finally managed to add, "Dad?"

"He cannot respond. He no longer breathes," my stepmother stated in her calm, gravelly voice.

I tried to sit up, but I couldn't.

"I'm trapped." My voice was shrill. I was trapped, and my father was dead. I began coughing again. I hadn't been crushed, but I couldn't straighten up in the space left by the rubble. My knees ached, bent so sharply and pushed against the cold hard floor with only the thin fabric of my nightgown in between.

"Be still child," replied Arla-Mia. Dad had explained that she was able to express more emotions in her native voice than we could with ours, but the mechanical nature of the voice box didn't transmit them well. Sometimes it was hard to remember I wasn't talking to a robot.

Her voice was closer now. I could hear the rubble being shifted—metal bending and concrete crashing to the side.

"I'm here." I said more quietly, taking a careful breath.

I began to shiver. Fresh air blew through the hallway from the roof. So cold. It must be air from outside the dome. Whatever pinned my torso down was shifted out of the way.

Three of her mottled blue-green tentacles lifted me clear of the floor and then I was in Arla-Mia's arms, being held close. When we moved into the dome, she had taken to hiding her tentacles under her clothing. It was easy to forget how strong she was. I clung to her, pushing my face into the slick skin of her neck and inhaling her familiar lemon tang.

Arla-Mia made soft reassuring humming sounds, in her natural voice. I peered around her shoulder as we moved back down the hall toward where I had last seen Dad, but I didn't want to see my father crushed under slabs of concrete.

I had a moment of horror as I realized where she was taking me. I hadn't even thought of my baby half-sister, likely sleeping when the tremors began. Arla-Mia neatly navigated us through the crumbled remains of the hall-way back toward her daughter's room. I strained to hear the baby crying.

After Isabel was born, I had tried to explain to Arla-Mia the difference between Mother and Step-mother. She understood that my birth-mother was no longer alive. She understood that she raised me now. She had always listened patiently, made time for me. She had been a stepmother to me, but I had thought maybe I was simply someone she was kind to. But she had saved me even before checking on her own baby. I watched her face, holding tight as we crossed the threshold into Isabel's debris-choked room.

Arla-Mia set me down on the floor just inside. I tried to stand, but my legs were wobbly from shock and wouldn't hold my weight. I slid back to the floor and set to rubbing some strength back into my calves.

My father and Arla-Mia had worked together for more than a year, two linguists untangling commu-nication between two species. When he told me he had fallen in love with an alien, I hadn't known what to think. When they announced their intention to attempt to have a child, there was a full-on media frenzy. All sorts of paranoid experts poured out of the woodwork claiming great risks to the human race if it was permitted.

Our home here under the dome was the compromise. I think Arla-Mia preferred the privacy and the climate control it permitted. For me, it meant finishing high school via remote classes and being isolated from my friends.

When Isabel was born she was a miracle. Her skin and vocal chords were human, but she had additional tentacles around her torso like her mother. She had her mother's sensitivity to cold, and her skin tone was closest to the green shades of the skin on my stepmother's scalp. Arla-Mia had no hair, but Isabel's hair was like mine—dark and tightly coiled.

Arla-Mia's tentacles whirled as she shifted furniture and slabs of ceiling out of her path. She kept her eyes on the center of the room where last night a delicate crib had stood. A noise turned us both toward the closet beside me. A muffled whimper.

I struggled to my feet and looked inside. The closet

was so dark. "Isabel?"

The ground began to shake again. I looked back towards Arla-Mia. I was looking right at her when the rest of the ceiling fell on her.

I stood in the closet's door frame, numb, tears sliding down my face, staring at the spot where until a moment ago my stepmother had stood. The aftershock faded quickly. Isabel's renewed cry from behind me broke my paralysis. I wasn't alone. Someone needed me.

I stepped all the way into the dark of the closet, reaching my hands above me and called her name again. When I felt the first tentative touch of one of her tentacles, I was surprised by their warmth against my fingertips.

She was strong and agile for being so little—a week shy of her first birthday. She swung down from the top shelf of the closet, wrapping one tentacle after the other around my arms—walking down my body. As she drew even with my face, she gently traced the salty paths of my tears and nuzzled into my shoulder. I held her tiny warm body close. "Were you scared?"

"La-La" She whispered into my neck. She hadn't mastered my name yet.

"Yes. It's me." I turned around and stared out at the

devastation in the room beyond. We stood in the dark of the closet. My feet were freezing. I was wearing a nightgown. Isabel was in nothing but a diaper.

A high pitched keening called to us from the room, from underneath a pile of plaster and boards. Isabel wriggled in my arms.

"No, Isabel. I will take you. Stay with me." She quieted as I picked my way back to the center of the room. I tried not to wince with each bare step on the uneven floor. "Arla-Mia, we are coming."

The keening shifted to an even hum, and we found her, her face peering out from between two beams. I knelt low so Isabel could reach out to her mother. I had never seen my stepmother cry. I wasn't sure she could. But my years of living with her had taught me to read her face, and I could see sorrow written across her features.

She said something I didn't understand to Isabel. Isabel replied in a sing-song sad voice.

Arla-Mia managed to place one tentacle over my heart.

"Stepmother now," she whispered as an alien hovercraft came into view above us. "Promise."

"I promise." I looked up at the large craft that was

lowering rescuers before turning back to her. "Maybe they can save you?"

She closed her eyes and left me with her child.

Jeanne Kramer-Smyth is an archivist by day and a writer, glass artist and fan of board games by night.

The Wolf Is Coming

Hope Erica Schultz

There was graffiti on the gray cinderblock wall again, splashed in a rusty-brown that looked like dried blood. *The Wolf Is Coming.*

Sarah was careful not to turn her head to look at it. She kept her eyes lowered on her bucket as she joined the line for water.

Both of the Deputies were there, today. Cyrus was chewing his mustache, his stubby fingers fidgeting on his gun, and Luke shuffled his feet and glared out at the crowd. The whispering in the line dried up to silence at the front, and no one made eye contact.

She focused on breathing slowly and evenly as the plodding line brought her closer. Five people in front of her, four, three …

When her turn came she ducked her head still further and lifted her bucket to the spigot. A hand tightened on her arm and she froze.

"Look at me, girl."

She raised her eyes carefully to Cyrus's chin, covered

127

in the scruffy blond beard that never seemed to fill in.

The hand tightened enough to hurt. "Look at me!"

She forced her eyes up and saw herself reflected in his mirrored glasses, a thin dark girl in patchwork clothes, cowering. She hated herself in that moment almost more than she hated him, but she kept her expression blank and open.

"You know who the Wolf is, girl?"

"No, sir."

"You'd tell me if you knew?"

"Yes, sir." She let her weak eye stray in just a little, and he dropped her arm, motioning her on. She lowered her eyes to the bucket, filled it mechanically, and turned back with it on the broken path towards home.

Who was the Wolf? Why was he, she, it coming? And if she knew, would she tell—would she tell anyone?

Home had been larger once. They'd had a twelve by twelve foot room in the old Mall soon after the War, a fabric store. After Dad had died she hadn't been able to defend it, and had left with what she could carry. Now she had a cobbled hut of mismatched pieces of plywood, brick, and corrugated metal. Sometimes she had a roommate, sometimes not. Now was a not time.

She drank before she portioned the rest of the water out; a jar in case tomorrow's water didn't come, then the smaller jar for the rest of today. She poured a drizzle of water over the potato plants just outside, then the remainder into the pot that served either for cooking or washing fabric. Which she did with it today depended on what she could get in trade.

The winds were rising when she headed over to Jim's. He had dug up most of the broken asphalt around his area over the years and built a low wall that marked a semi-official market space. Today there were a handful of strangers with the usual farmers and crafters, and Sarah tightened her hold on her goods.

Jim called out to her as she approached. "Anything new, Miss Sarah?" He smiled, splitting his wide, dark face and showing the handful of gold teeth amongst the white.

Sarah fought and failed to suppress a smile. "A shirt, today," she offered. "If you know anyone who might be buying."

"I might. You interested in a roommate for a few days? Fellow here who would rather not be out in the rain we're likely to get in a few hours." Jim nodded towards a teenage boy her age or a little older who was standing by the low wall. His clothes were scuffed and torn but relatively clean; he was slender—who wasn't?—and his features were sharp with a triangular face and a square chin that emphasized the pallor of his skin. His eyes were blue, and he smiled much like Jim did.

Sarah frowned. That Jim thought he was safe was no guarantee, but rent would be welcome. She walked straight to the stranger, holding eye contact. "How long are you planning on staying?"

"A few days, probably. I'll pay by the day."

Sarah nodded. "What are you offering?"

He smiled again as he held out a freshly skinned rabbit in his left hand. "Half of this, for today. I can hunt more, or I can do labor for the rest."

Sarah tried to think when she'd last had meat. "I'm renting space only. You try to touch me, I'll kill you."

His eyes smiled, but his expression turned serious. "Fair enough. I'm Max." He held out his right hand.

"Sarah." She clasped his hand, warm in the cool of the afternoon. "I'll show you the place as soon as I finish my sales here."

The shirt sold for a pound of dried beans, a cured rabbit skin, and the ragged green garment it was replacing. Sarah traded the skin for several yard strands of thread, a needle, and a fragment of yellow cloth about a foot square. She nodded to Max as she left, and he followed without a word.

Max took off his shoes on entering the hut and settled cross legged on one of the yoga mats she used as both flooring and mattress. She busied herself lighting the fire under the pot of water and then turned back to him.

"Where are you from?"

"Before, or since?" His smile was easy, and he settled back slightly. "I grew up outside Boston, before. I was in the Saint V's settlement after the war."

Ten miles away. Sarah frowned, vaguely remembering when cars and buses had made that a short distance. "Why did you leave?"

"The Wolf came."

The words seemed to echo, and Sarah flinched, glancing around instinctively for witnesses. "What happened?" she whispered.

Max smiled as though they were discussing a sunny day, or the rabbit about to be cooked. "Change."

A dog was barking when Sarah woke the next morning. The sound of breaking glass made her scramble to her feet.

"It's tax day," she explained tersely to Max. He sat up, frowning.

"When do you have tax day?"

"Whenever the Guard feels like it." She lined the yoga mats up neatly and checked that needle and thread strands were both woven into her clothing with nothing showing. She'd picked the green shirt apart into pieces the night before, and the beans were already soaking in the leftover stew. There was a moment of panic in the realization that while there was nothing they were likely to take … there was also nothing to appease them. Reluctantly she pulled the small blanket she'd been piecing together out of the rag pile and folded it neatly on top of her mat.

She glanced over at Max, who now sat cross legged on his mat. She opened her mouth to warn him then shut it and gestured to him to stand. She could hear Cyrus talking next door, a rumble of threat with no distinguishable words.

Her eyes dropped to the floor as her makeshift door was flung open. Three pairs of boots showed that the Guard had come himself, today.

"What do you have for me, girl?" Cyrus grabbed her chin, while Luke dumped Max's pack onto the nearest mat.

Sarah swallowed her fear and indicated the blanket. Cyrus gathered it up and tossed it to the Guard, who examined it and nodded. Max's pack produced little beyond some questionable meat jerky and a collection of twine and sticks. A small green bottle had no stopper and was too small to be useful; his canteen was dented and rusted.

"That all you got, boy?" Luke asked, and Max smiled, meeting his gaze.

"I'm told I've got my health and good looks."

Luke glanced at the Guard, who stepped forward to pick up the bottle. He held it up to the light by the door and smiled as he smashed it against a cinderblock.

"Have better for me next time if you want water," he said, and then nodded to Luke. Luke grinned as he turned the gun to jam the stock into Max's unprotected stomach, then the three men left.

Sarah held her breath for a moment before sinking to her knees. She gathered up the pieces of the green bottle then looked over at Max. He was holding his stomach, but smiling, like a rifle stock to the gut was funny. She sat back, shaking her head.

"Why didn't you look away?"

Max raised one eyebrow. "Because they don't

scare me. They're just people; just bullies like you'll find anywhere."

"They should scare you. These bullies have guns."

Max stretched slightly, and winced. "It's been ten years. How many bullets do you think they have left? One shot gun, one rifle, and one hand gun. They didn't waste a bullet on me, did they?" He smiled again, and Sarah shook her head.

"You are one crazy bastard."

She meant it, and it was true, but it didn't keep her from smiling back.

The walls by the spigot helped to explain why the Guard and his men had been in such a foul mood. Each one had graffiti on it, in different scrawls or scratches. *The Wolf Is Here.*

Max had come with his canteen as she carried her bucket. A crowd was gathering, but no line was forming; the Guard and his deputies were standing in front of the spigot, weapons out.

"We'll have answers, now, or no water for any of you! Who is the Wolf?"

A rumble of consternation went through the crowd, then Max stepped forward. He was smiling again, Jim's smile, a smile that reminded her oddly of Before, of plentiful food and safety.

"I am the Wolf," he said.

There was a moment of shocked silence, and then Luke lifted his rifle to his shoulder and fired. Max fell to the ground, a hole blossoming in his head … and still smiling.

Sarah dropped to her knees beside him, searching the darkening eyes. He had known a secret, and she wanted it, wanted it more than she had ever wanted anything. Then, as the murmur began and she heard the Guard laugh, she found it.

"Well, now that that's taken care of," the Guard was saying as she rose back to her feet, tall and proud and unafraid.

"I am the Wolf!"

The Guard paused and Luke hesitantly began to raise his rifle again. She could feel the smile splitting her face, the joy of relinquishing her fear.

"I am the Wolf." It was Jim, and he too was smiling.

Luke shifted his hold on the gun and Cyrus raised his. A woman Sarah didn't know straightened suddenly, face serene. "I am the Wolf."

"I am the Wolf!" The chant was growing now, voices

overlapping.

How many bullets do you think they have?

Not enough, apparently. Luke broke first, and then Cyrus and the Guard were turning with him, turning to run.

"I am the Wolf!"

They were still running when the crowd pulled them down and tore them apart.

Hope Erica Schultz lives in Central Massachusetts with her spouse, two children, one dog, four cats, and assorted visiting wildlife. She writes SF and fantasy stories and novels that can be considered comedy, adventure, or horror depending on where she chooses to end them. When not writing, reading, or pretending to be someone else, she still works for a living. Find her at https://www.facebook.com/hope.schultz.14

Death and Taxes
C.H. Spalding

You wake up to the alarm like it's an ordinary morning. The coverall feels cool on your skin as you pull it on; it's getting a little short in the legs, but there's no sense in worrying about that now.

Susan is already in the kitchen. She doesn't look as though she's slept at all, and as much as you don't want to, you feel a little sorry for her. She doesn't have many more choices than you do, and everyone always says that blood is thicker than water.

Why do they say that? It isn't water that's scarce—it's air.

"Would you mind getting your sister up?" she asks, already busy cooking breakfast. You see that she is making French toast, like it's your birthday or something.

Or something.

You shake your head and go to your sister's compartment. You never addressed Susan as "Mom," not even when she first married Dad when you were little, but today it feels almost cruel to call her by her first name.

Cara is starting to wake up when you lift her out, and she wraps her arms around you. She's talking, a little now, and goes to the crèche a lot more while Susan works. You usually watch her in the evenings until Susan gets home.

In one more month, you'd be done with school and working enough for your social credits and the rest of the family, beside. The taxes, unfortunately, are due now. With Dad dead, Susan just doesn't make enough to support three people.

Susan hands you a plate as you return to the kitchen, and you look at her, trying to remember why you used to hate her.

"I asked if we could leave Cara at the crèche, today, but the whole family has to be there."

You nod. The rules always make at least a twisted kind of sense. Your family had been lucky enough never to have to face this, before, but luck was as scarce as air, with never enough to go around.

You eat in silence, enjoying the flavors, and then force a smile. "Thank you."

Susan nods, but doesn't smile back. "You're welcome."

There are things you could bring with you, but there's no sense, really. You stare at your single shelf of belongings, at your reflection in the small mirror, and then close the door to your compartment. Cara can have your things, and your room, when she's older.

Cara is fussing, and you take her from your step-mother and rest her against one hip. "I'll carry her."

Susan's severe face softens a little, even though she doesn't smile. "Thank you."

You head out into the corridor, knowing from the noises behind that Susan is following. You pass the turn to your class, the turn to the infirmary, and follow the corridor to the very back of the ship.

There are only two families waiting outside the ac-counting room. One stands in angry silence, not look-ing at each other. One family is crying and hugging and carrying on so that you are actually a little embar-rassed. Then there are the three of you, a small broken family about to get smaller.

You bounce Cara on your hip and talk to her as you wait, ignoring the other families. At length the door opens, and a woman comes out calling Susan's name as head of household.

You walk inside, trying not to hold Cara too tightly, with Susan right behind you. You've never been here before, and the room is small and sterile and cold, with three doors including the one you came in through. The woman who summoned you in has returned to her computer; there are two guards behind her, both armed.

"Susan Evans, you do not have enough social credits to cover the air for three people. As head of household you must designate the member to be withdrawn. You have five minutes," the woman says, as though five minutes now will make any difference. The door on the back wall is frosted, and you look at it, refusing to flinch.

You've known what had to happen ever since Dad had his accident. You might not have been an easy stepchild, but you love Cara as much as any full sibling could.

You turn to hand Cara back to Susan, but she is glaring at you fiercely, and then puts a hand on either side of your face.

"I didn't always like you ... but I didn't have to like you to love you."

She touches her forehead to yours, puts a hand on Cara's curls like a benediction, then turns and walks to the airlock door, and through it.

C. H. Spalding has been writing short stories since the 1980s or before. Only claim to fame: having dinner with Anne McCaffrey in 1992, then nervously pushing her in a wheelchair around the Atlanta airport to get her to her flight. She wanted to take the escalator at one point. Oh God, the terror.

The Wolf Listens

Madeline Smoot

She of the Impure Heart sat by the small campfire, waiting. She took in deep breaths of the fire's acrid smoke, faintly perfumed with the kitchen herbs she had stolen. The older student who had told her in whispers and half muffled snatches about the ceremony had mentioned sacred, magical herbs for the ritual. He just couldn't tell her from those half-remembered tales from his youth which herbs to use. Impure Heart could only hope that rosemary, basil and coriander would suffice.

A small breeze pulled at Impure Heart's nightdress and blew more smoke from the fire into her face. Impure felt odd outside without a corset and the stiff starched collars of her uniform, but she had not wanted to meet an Animal of her ancestors garbed in the day clothes the white men of the school chose for her to wear. Her traditional clothes along with her family, her language, and her name had all been taken from her the day she had arrived at the School, eleven years before.

With her long hair braided down her back instead of pinned on top of her head, and despite the bright white nightdress instead of soft leathers, Impure hoped she looked more like her proud mother and less like the meek servant girl the School had trained her to be. Perhaps if she succeeded tonight, that meek little servant girl would no longer exist.

Hunger gnawed painfully at her. She had never gone an entire day without food before. It was perhaps the only good thing that could be said about the School: no child there starved. The older student had warned her that her *Hembleciya* could take many days and that she would not be able to eat at all during that time. The boy had looked fearful and a bit daring when he had whispered the forbidden word, *Hembleciya*. He had looked over his shoulder, afraid a teacher might hear him speaking something other than English.

Impure's stomach grumbled again, and she hoped an Animal would appear this night. She had barely managed all of her chores and lessons today. She could not imagine doing them after a second day without food. Perhaps fasting was not necessary. After all, how much could the boy really know about this? He was only two years older; they had both left the tribe on the same day. He was no adult ... here words failed her. She did not know the right term for the holy men of her tribe. She rubbed her eyes, wiping away tears she had not shed in years.

She did not see the Animal step into the firelight, so she had no knowledge of how long he stood studying her before she noticed him. In human form, he stood taller than any mortal man she had ever seen, almost towering over the saplings around them. Nearly naked, the only thing he wore was a headdress made from the head and skin of a wolf.

A wolf.

She had been sent Wolf.

Impure had been hoping to see the mischievous smile of Coyote or perhaps the strength of Bear. Predatory and fierce as Wolf might be, she did not see how he could help her. She tried to hide her dismay, but some must have leaked onto her face or into her scent carried by the traitorous wind.

Wolf took a great sniff, and then he moved around the fire a step closer. "I am not your first choice?"

Impure felt her face flush, and not from the heat of the fire. She was not so ignorant as to think she could pick her own Animal as if ordering off a menu in the white men's fancy restaurants. She remembered that much at least from her short time with her family.

Wolf did not seem to expect a response. He studied her for another moment before holding out his hand. "Come."

Impure shrunk back a little. The entire palm of her hand wouldn't cover the pad of a single one of his fingers. She had known that she might be taken on a journey, set on a new path as part of the ritual, but the idea of travelling with this Animal, with this God, terrified her.

"Come," Wolf said again. "I will not devour you."

Impure would have found it more comforting if he had promised her no harm. She chewed on the inside of her cheek for a moment, and then began to reach out her hand. Wasn't this why she had called the Animals? For their aid? At the last moment, before she had quite touched him, she paused. "Shouldn't," she began. Her voice cracked, and she had to take a deep breath before she began again. "Shouldn't I tell you what I want?"

Wolf bared his teeth in a particularly lupine smile. It sat oddly on his otherwise human face. "I will show you what you need."

Impure placed her hand on his.

Wolf pulled on her hand, lifting her spirit from

her body. Impure was surprised to find that it didn't hurt more than rubbing a brush across the back of an arm. How odd to see herself still sitting, staring at the fire. Did her ears really look like that? She had never seen herself from the side and only rarely in a mirror. The School forbade looking glasses since they believed such things led to vanity.

While she stood staring at herself, Wolf had shifted into his animal form. Impure shivered, disconcerted by the change. She had thought the huge human intimidating. She found the wolf towering a full head over her terrifying.

"Come," he said for the final time. "Ride on me."

Impure's spirit legs went weak. Taking the Wolf-man's hand had been hard enough. She suspected she didn't possess the courage to climb on this creature's back.

Wolf sniffed, clearly scenting her fear. "Where we go, you cannot walk. You must ride or all of this will have been for nothing."

Impure Heart thought about the hunger, the spice theft, and the trouble she had endured trying to sneak out of her room in the dead of night. She didn't want to have to do those things again. She wanted to be free, and she wanted to be free tonight. Gathering her re-solve to her chest the way a mother gathers her child, Impure Heart scrambled and slid and finally pulled herself onto the Animal.

The moment she had shifted into place, Wolf trotted away from the fire and Impure's body. Impure looked back once. Her physical form had not moved since her spirit had been lifted away. It sat there, watching the fire, patiently waiting for her to return.

Wolf began to steadily climb a mountain although there were no mountains within several hundred miles of the School. Never breaking his stride or changing his speed, Wolf navigated steep inclines and switch-backed trails with ease. They had been climbing for no more than a few minutes, yet they had covered many miles of ground. Wolf's speed left Impure breathless.

"Why do you refer to yourself as that? As Impure Heart? It is not your given name."

Impure Heart's gaze snapped from the side of the mountain to the wolf head in front of her. She had not expected such a question. She snorted as her first re-sponse. Then realizing how rude that sounded, she quickly answered, "I was not given my name. It was assigned my first day at the School. The matron said I 'looked like a Catherine' whatever a Catherine is. I am not Catherine."

"That is not what I meant," said Wolf. "I meant the name given to you at birth."

Impure Heart looked down at her hands, clutching Wolf's fur. "I do not know that name," she said at last. "When I first started at the school, I had trouble remembering the name, Catherine. The matron told me to say, 'I am Catherine,' twenty times every night. She sat with me while I did it. I never became Catherine, but I did cease to be ... someone else."

Wolf gave a grumbled growl in what might have been sympathy or might have been disgust. "That does not explain the impure heart," he said.

Impure Heart continued to stare at her hands. Even though she knew it to be impossible, she felt Wolf's gaze on her, and she could not meet his eyes.

"A few years after I started, a preacher came to the School. He was horrified to learn that although we attended services daily, most of us had not been baptized. After we had been wetted, he pronounced us clean of sin and pure of heart. But even then, at that young age, I knew it to be a lie. I wished for nothing more than for the Christian God to strike the School and the preacher and to burn them with the hellfire the preacher spoke so often about. My heart is not pure."

A silence descended between Impure and the Wolf. It was not the companionable silence of friends, nor the awkward silence of strangers. This silence filled the night with Wolf's disapproval. They continued to climb the mountain. The fire with Impure's physical body, shrank away until it was merely another star in the landscape.

"Why did you wish for Coyote or Bear?" Wolf finally asked.

"I had hoped that Coyote would trick the School into releasing me or that Bear would come and with great strength knock the school away."

"Coyote would have achieved your goal, but the trick would have been on you."

"What do you mean?" asked Impure with a frown.

"Coyote would have filled you with child."

Impure wrinkled her nose. That would have gotten her removed from the School, that was certainly true. She wasn't sure though that she wanted a child now.

"But Bear could still have smashed the School," said Impure. Her eyes lit up as she imagined the massive Animal stomping on buildings and knocking down trees.

"You know nothing of Bear."

Impure sat back sharply as if she had been stung by Wolf's words. She did not need his reminder that she knew nothing about her culture.

"That is not how Bear solves problems," continued Wolf, apparently unaware of Impure's embarrassment, "and even if she did knock down your school, do you really see the white men allowing such a deed to go unpunished?"

Impure paused. Wolf had a point. Only last year the newspapers had been filled with tales of the massacre back home. The teachers had shook their heads and sighed and told the students how lucky they were to be safe at the School. Impure knew their safety to be a lie. No student had ever been shot, that was true, but students who had succumbed to illness filled the small cemetery behind the back gate.

Although she didn't think that any of her close kin had died, she would have preferred to be one of those killed in the massacre with family rather than one of the students who died alone in the infirmary's bed.

"We have arrived," said Wolf. "You may climb down."

Even though they were a tremendous height up, Impure wasn't cold, even in just a simple nightdress.

Her fingers were not stiff as she unwound them from Wolf's fur. She climbed down onto the rocky surface, but the sharp rocks didn't poke or cut at her spirit's bare feet.

Still in his animal form, Wolf led Impure to the edge of the mountain. Spread out below like a drawing or a map lay the School and beyond it a town. The School with its walls and uniform buildings reminded Impure of a prison.

"Look," said Wolf. "Tell me what you see."

"The School and the town," said Impure, "from very far away. I wish they would stay far away."

Wolf shook his head. "You are looking only with your eyes. Tell me what you see."

Matron, back down in the School, often said that God worked in mysterious ways. Apparently the same was true of the Animals. How was she supposed to see beyond her eyes?

Impure stared down at the buildings she hated, symbolic of a life she loathed. She tried as hard as she could, using more than her eyes. She stared so long without blinking that the white buildings below began to turn into amorphous blobs that then started swirling together. The white seemed to drain away from the scene like the water flushing down the kitchen sink's drain. Only varying shades of brown were left upon the landscape. Slowly the brown blobs began to re-form not only into *tipis* from her childhood but also into *asi*, *adobe*, and grass houses. For the students at the School came from many different nations, and all of the children brought their heritage with them, whether they remembered it or not.

"You begin to see," said Wolf. "Look closer."

Impure leaned farther over the edge. The ground seemed to draw closer as if she now possessed an eagle's eye. Individual students slept in their historic homes, dreaming of moments from their past, moments Impure would have sworn they had forgotten.

"It's all still here," she murmured, more to herself than to Wolf. "We are still ourselves."

"Yes," said Wolf.

"But we are still trapped," said Impure. She turned away from the scene before her to stare in Wolf's eyes instead. "We remain confined to this school."

Wolf growled. "Still you do not see. Perhaps this will help." Faster than Impure's eyes could follow, faster than a human could move, Wolf used his haunches to shove Impure off the edge of the mountain.

Impure fell forward with a scream, flailing her arms in a futile attempt to save herself. Only her arms no longer existed. Instead two wings began to beat steadily at her side. The feet tucked under her body no longer ended in toes but taloned claws. Her eyes really had become those of an eagle. The panicked beating of her heart subsided as she flew.

Beside her, Wolf ran in the sky; his feet pounding on a path only he could see. Impure felt glad of his company. As wonderful, as freeing, as flying made her feel, she would have felt isolated doing it alone.

"Why do you persist in being alone?" asked Wolf. "The School you attend restricts you physically, yes, but the prison you speak of is the one you built around yourself."

Impure veered away from the invisible path Wolf ran and soared around in the air, circling once, twice over the School. It had returned to its usual white brick façade. She tried to fly away from Wolf's words, but she knew that he was right. Since the day she had taken Impure Heart for her name, she had withdrawn from the others, too busy plotting impossible plans of escape to worry with friends.

She circled one more time around the school and

then lit on a branch in a tree near the fire where her physical body still sat, staring into the flames.

Wolf, back in human form, stood next to the tree, his eyes level with hers. "In that School," he said, "lives a boy who whispers the words of your native tongue to himself every night so that he will not forget them. There is a girl who keeps a Winter Count drawn on a page hidden in her room. There is another boy who writes down the stories his grandfather used to tell him in the evenings."

"Do you think the boy, the one who whispers, do you think he would teach me some words?" Impure held her breath, fearful of the answer.

"I think you should ask," said Wolf, in his inscrutable way. He held out a finger for Impure to perch on. "It is time for us to return, *Zitkala*."

Impure stepped on his finger, her head cocked birdlike to one side. "That is not my name."

"Not the one you were born with, nor the one given at the School, no, but it is your name nonetheless."

Impure said nothing, chewing over the new name in her head as he lowered her towards the fire.

Wolf helped her spirit settle back into her body. Impure blinked once, and once more, her eyes refocusing on the fire before her. Of the Wolf, there was nothing to be seen. Except for a single eagle's feather clutched in her hand, there was no sign that he had ever been there.

Impure Heart slowly pulled herself to her feet. The stiffness she had not felt on the cold mountain had appeared. She could barely bring her legs to straighten. She began the long walk back to the School, with a heart a little lighter than when she had left there earlier in the night.

Tomorrow she would find the boy and have him whisper words of their language to her. But first she would ask him the meaning of her new name.

Madeline Smoot writes, edits, and talks about children's books pretty much all day every day. It's kind of annoying for family and friends. Join her for a chat about writing and editing kid books on her website at www.buriededitor.com.